MISTLETOE PROMISE

A CHRISTMAS WISHING WELL NOVELLA

SOFI LAPORTE

http://www.sofilaporte.com
sofi@sofilaporte.com

c/o Block Services
Stuttgarter Str. 106
70736 Fellbach, Germany

Editor: Caroline Barnhil.
Cover Art: Covers and Cupcakes.

ISBN: 978-3-9505190-0-6

❀ Created with Vellum

For all teachers, our unsung heroes

CHAPTER 1

*O*ne single snowflake.

The tiny crystal floated through the grey sky, twirled about like a ballerina in a white fluffy frock, drifted over the trees, danced down the gables of a stately mansion and clung to its windowpane, where it melted to a drop of ice water, sliding down like a teardrop.

Frances touched the cold glass with a finger and traced down its path. Lifting her eyes, she saw that it was growing dark outside. In the glimmer of the streetlamp, she saw a host of snowflakes whirling about before they powdered the ground.

She ought to light her lamp, too. It was also getting cold in the room. She got up and placed another log into the fireplace. It sparked. Frances took the bellows and stoked up the fire. Normally, it was the maid's job to do this, but these were strange times. Both housemaids were unavailable. Betty had left to get married several days earlier, Martha had come down with the flu, and Mrs Beedle, the cook, had begged a leave of absence to tend to her mother, who had fallen ill as well. Somehow, word had got out that Martha had measles, which had caused the parents and guardians of the pupils to break out in panic. Despite Frances's protestations to the contrary, they pulled their children from school a week prior to the holidays.

Frances sighed. She wondered what Miss Hilversham would've done in this situation. The headmistress of Miss Hilversham's Seminary for Young Ladies, which also carried her name, was absent as well. She was visiting a former pupil, the former Miss Birdie Talbot, who was now the Duchess of Dunross. She'd begged Miss Hilversham to help her set up a school in Scotland. Miss Hilversham had agreed, and transferred the running of the school, including all of its administerial duties, to Frances. From the initially planned two months, it stretched to three, and now Christmas was approaching and there was no sign of Miss Hilversham returning.

It is likely I will stay over the holidays in Scotland, she'd written in her last missive. *It is nigh impossible to travel now, with the snow blocking most of the roads. I would be quite worried about this predicament if I did not know the school in such capable hands as yours, dear Frances.*

Frances folded the letter with a frown. There was no work to do these days since all the students had left. Normally, there was a forlorn soul or two to tend to over the holidays. Frances had looked forward to a small celebration; she'd been prepared to pamper whoever had not been so lucky to leave the school over Christmastide. But all the students had left, no doubt because she hadn't been able to quench the rumour about the false measles.

The teachers were gone as well. Of the four teachers

who taught in the school, not counting the headmistress, Miss Robinson and Miss Brown had left to visit their families over the holidays, and Miss Keating had resigned the day before.

Frances alone remained.

The house was eerily quiet. Gone were the footsteps in the hallway, the scraping of chalk on the blackboards, the shuffling of papers and books, the scraping of quills.

With the house empty of all human sounds, others became prevalent. The wind that howled around the gables. The squeaking of the broken shutter on the upper floor. The mysterious creaking of the floorboards upstairs.

Frances held her breath as she listened. Maybe it was Martha walking around? She ought to be in bed. She pulled her plaid shawl tighter across her shoulder and shivered.

Was she to celebrate Christmas all on her own, then?

With a sigh, Frances placed the letter back in the letter box. It was too dark to read or write. It was too cold to be up and about. She would wrap herself in another shawl, pull over a second pair of thick woollen socks, go down to the kitchen to get a pot of hot tea and crawl into her bed.

Tomorrow will be a new day.

A sudden banging against the front door exploded through the house.

Frances jumped. Her heart pounded.

There again. Bam. Bam. Bam. Insistent. Authoritative.

And now the bell jangled.

Who could that be?

It was the twenty-first of December, St Thomas day, so maybe it was a poor woman, a mumper, who, as was custom on that day, went from house to house, applying to the goodwill of the people, begging for alms. She'd opened her door to more than one mumper already and given them food parcels consisting of bread, cake, and a coin. But all of them had tapped discreetly on the kitchen door, not the main entrance.

She waited one moment for Martha to open the door until she remembered that Martha was lying upstairs in a fever. There would be no one else to open the door. She was all alone.

Frances shivered and for one moment considered ignoring the summons. Surely, it wasn't a mumper. Who else could it be in this weather? Surely no one important? Miss Hilversham's missives of the day had been delivered. All the students were gone. It certainly was no parent.

And yet.

And yet, she was left in charge here. It could be someone important. It could be a courier. An urgent letter... Frances got up, pulled the shawl tighter around her shoulder, grabbed her candle and went downstairs.

The old walnut clock ticked in the hallway, shadows flitted to and fro, the open doors of the classrooms looked like gawking black mouths.

Bam. Bam. Bam. Followed by the bell pull.

"I'm coming, I'm coming," Frances muttered under her breath in the same way Martha did, especially on busy visiting days.

She reached the front door, turned the heavy key in the lock, and pushed down the latch.

She was pushed back by the weight of a man's body who'd been leaning against the door.

Frances jumped back with a squeak, holding her candle up in defence as the man stumbled forward.

"I–I beg your pardon. Didn't expect the door to open so suddenly." He drew himself up and adjusted the hat on his head. He was tall and lanky with ash blond hair stuck to his temples. His eyes glistened.

Frances took another step back, wishing she'd taken with her the poker stick from the fireplace before she went downstairs. "W–w–we have no more alms." Where was Martha when one needed her the most? Prostrate in bed.

He drew his tongue over cracked lips. "I want no alms." His hand went into the breast pocket of his greatcoat.

If he draws out a pistol, I will throw the candlestick at him, Frances thought wildly. She looked around for another weapon.

Instead of a pistol, he pulled out something that crinkled. Frances raised her candlestick, ready to strike.

"I am here for this–" he held out his hand, in which he held a piece of paper.

Frances stared at it.

His hand wavered.

Just in the moment that Frances reached out to take it, his hand trembled, dropping the paper.

With a crash, he collapsed at her feet.

He'd fainted.

Outside, snowflakes drifted and twirled about in a hectic winter dance.

CHAPTER 2

Frances stared at the prostrate man, perplexed. He lay face down, his legs were halfway out the door, his coat sprawled about him, his top hat had rolled into the hall and lay at the foot of a mahogany long case clock. A draught of icy wind blew into the house. In the shock of the moment, the only coherent thought Frances could form was "It's snowing into the house, I'd better close the door."

She shook herself. Then she placed the candle on a side table, knelt on the floor, and gave his shoulder a nudge.

"Sir? Is everything all right? Are you dead?" Stupid question. If he were dead, he'd hardly reply. And he wouldn't be lying by her feet if he were all right. But what to do?

Her mind worked feverishly.

She nudged him again. No sound.

"Very well. Then I have to move you." Taking him

under the armpits, she attempted to pull him farther into the hallway.

"Sweet heavens, you're heavy," Frances grunted. She slipped on the carpet and landed on her bottom. This gave her an idea. Maybe she could pull the carpet he was lying on. That proved to work somewhat better. She managed, after a lot of huffing and puffing, to manoeuvre the body into the reception room on the right. After she deposited him on the floor next to the sofa, she returned to the hall, closed the door and picked up the candle. He still lay with his face down. With a grunt and a heave, she turned him on his back.

The man was definitely unconscious.

He wasn't inebriated, as she had initially thought. His skin burned underneath her touch. He was ill. He had a fever.

"What now?" She'd managed to drag him into the reception room. She would not be able to heave him onto the sofa. He was far too heavy.

What did one do when one had a fever?

Frances left to get a bowl of cool water, a cloth, a glass of water and some smelling salts. She wiped his forehead with a cold, wet cloth. He stirred and muttered.

"Oh good. So you aren't dead. I must say, that's a relief. What am I to do with you, however? I can't leave you on the floor? Not if you're ill?"

He muttered some more.

She held the smelling salts under his nose.

He stirred.

Frances lifted the glass with water and wet his lips. His eyelids fluttered, and he stirred, then he drank the water with greedy gulps.

"Good, that's it. Slowly. There."

"…position," he muttered.

"I'm sorry, I don't understand. Can you repeat that?"

"M here for the position." He looked around, disoriented. "Paper?"

Frances remembered that he'd been trying to show her a slip of paper before he'd fainted. She found it on the floor in the hallway and picked it up.

She recognised it as being an excerpt, an advertisement from *The Times*, which Miss Hilversham had posted several weeks ago.

Exclusive private Seminary for Young Ladies in Bath is seeking a single, respectable, dependable, highly educated gentleman or gentlewoman for instructing Latin, history and drawing. He or she has been expressly educated for this purpose and has the necessary references. Only serious contacts please…..

Frances wrinkled her brow. "Did you mean to apply for a teaching position?"

The man pulled himself up to his elbows.

"Yes. I'd like to apply for this position." He placed a hand on the coffee table and pulled himself up. Swaying, he made a half-bow.

"Miss Hilversham is not here." Frances's mind worked. "The school is closed, and the next term won't start until after Christmastide," she added.

"I must insist that you give me this position." He swayed once more. His eyes were enormous, round and glistening.

"Well." Frances looked around helplessly, but of course there was no one she could ask. She was all alone, she was responsible, she was representing the headmistress in her absence. "I am sure we can discuss this matter when Miss Hilversham has returned. Until then–"

"I need the position now." He swayed dangerously towards her.

"You'd better sit before you collapse again," Frances held out her hands, alarmed. She pushed him gently back, and he dropped onto the sofa behind him.

"… need the position now," he mumbled as he closed his eyes and leaned his head back.

His face was pale and narrow against the dark green velvet cover of the sofa. Strands of blond hair stuck to his brow. He looked very young. He had long eyelashes and a long, sensitive mouth.

He could be as old as Nat, it shot through Frances's mind.

A slight groan escaped his lips. "… position…" His voice cracked. "Please?"

Frances felt helpless when she saw the pleading look in his hazel eyes. What should she do? She could hardly send him away, out into this bleak winter night, when he was ill. She wouldn't even be able to get him on his feet. As for the position… As headmistress representative, Miss Hilversham had given her the authority to hire personnel, hadn't she?

"I trust you will find us a suitable replacement for Betty," she'd said. But hiring teachers wasn't quite the same as hiring a housemaid.

"We will talk about it later," Frances decided. "After you have rested."

Relief flushed over his face. "You are an angel," he whispered.

Then he fell into deep unconsciousness.

CHAPTER 3

*S*urely, angels did exist.

They came in all sorts of shapes, forms, and sizes, and they need not look particularly glamorous, either. This one, for example, barely reached his shoulder, had chestnut coloured hair, a round child-like face and the most expressive brown eyes he'd ever seen. There was also a halo, most definitely, a glow about her head that threw golden strands of highlight into her rich brown hair.

Maybe it was the candle that stood on the commode behind her. But no. This golden glow that engulfed her was no ordinary light. It was definitely a halo.

Where were the wings? He squinted and tried to lean on his elbows.

A hand pushed him back down.

"Want to see the wings," he mumbled.

He felt something on his lips, something cool. Water. He spluttered. He didn't want water. He wanted—he'd wanted something most desperately. Dash it if he hadn't forgotten what he wanted.

Ah yes. He remembered.

"Position," he mumbled.

"Yes, yes," the angel replied in her sweet voice. Gentle, soothing. Like her hand on his forehead. It brought a silly smile to his face. He could listen to that voice forever.

"Angel wings," he remembered. He wanted to study the angel wings. Did they have feathers? He must know, so he could paint them later.

Once more, a hand pushed him down.

"I think you'll feel better if you drink this."

He didn't want to drink anything. He wanted to see her angel wings.

Something hot and bitter poured down his throat. He spluttered.

"Willow bark tea," the sweet voice said. "Alas, we ran out of honey. Our housemaid is ill, too, and our cook hasn't had the opportunity to obtain more honey because she's with her ill mother." A sigh. "These are odd times. Everyone seems to be ill. I daresay it must be the weather, because the frost has come so suddenly."

He listened to the voice, enjoying her cadence, the slight lisp of her sibilants. It was childlike and suited her. She kept talking, but he'd long lost track of what she said. He listened, content, to the steady rhythm of her voice. It soothed him. The last time he'd felt like that was when he was ill with scarlet fever and his mother had sat by his bed the entire night. He'd nearly died. But then a miracle happened, and the fever had broken. He'd improved, but then his mother had succumbed to the same fever.

"Mother," he whispered.

"Oh no, no, no, I am not your mother." The voice sounded vaguely horrified. "I am not an angel, either. My name is Frances Littleworth, though no doubt you will forget that by the time you awake tomorrow morning. I teach music. I also assist the headmistress, Miss Hilversham. She is currently away, as I am sure I must have mentioned. I hope she hasn't fallen ill, as well. This cursed weather! Though I otherwise do like the snow. Especially at Christmas. Goodness, I seem to talk a lot. Blame it on not having had anyone to talk to these past few days. One turns rather peculiar. I suppose life as a hermit would never suit me."

She poured more of that horrid hot stuff down his throat.

"There. I daresay you will sleep now, and tomorrow we will talk anew, yes?"

His lids felt leaden. He could not move as much as his little toe. He wanted to thank the angel, but all that came out of his mouth was "Gnn."

Someone patted his hand.

He fell into a deep sleep.

Prove to me that you are capable of fending for yourself!
You have a talent, Percy. Promise me you will develop it.
You are no son of mine, you are a disgrace, I say. A disgrace!
I have all the confidence in you that in the end you will make
your own way. Always follow your heart.
You will end up in the gutter living with the rats, mark my
words.
Master Percy. Your mother is in heaven with the angels. I am so
very sorry.

Always follow your heart.
Always follow your heart.
Always follow your heart.

HIS SLEEP WAS FITFUL. HE WAS THRASHING ABOUT, throwing the blanket to the ground, groaning, twisting, turning on the narrow sofa. Once, Frances left for a short while to make tea, and when she returned, she found him halfway on the ground. Frances had pushed him back just before he toppled off the sofa entirely. She could not heave him back on the sofa on her own. She pushed two of the armchairs next to the sofa to prevent him from tumbling down.

He mumbled incoherently; the fever had him in full grip. Mother, he uttered more than once. Angel. Disgrace and heart.

Frances shook her head. Surely it was the fever speaking, not that he was mentally unstable. Although she did not get the initial impression that he was insane, one never knew. If he did not improve soon, she'd have to call a doctor.

Frances prayed that Mrs Beedle would return tomorrow, or that Martha recovered. If that failed, she'd have to ask Mrs Benningfield for help. Mr and Mrs Benningfield lived in the Grand Manor not too far from school. Mrs Benningfield was a kindly soul who enjoyed pampering students and teachers with baskets of sweets and fruits. She'd been a teacher herself once, she'd explained, and would have loved to continue teaching if it weren't for her seven children, who kept her busy. Frances knew she could apply to her anytime, and even Miss Hilversham had told her to turn to Mrs Benningfield for help should there be need.

With a frown, Frances looked down on the feverish man, who'd stopped thrashing around and was now sleeping with shallow breath.

She studied his face. He wasn't exactly handsome. But his forehead was proud and high, his ears well-shaped against his head, his lips finely lined, the chin firm. If there was something in his face that wasn't entirely harmonious with the rest, it would be his nose, which was slightly bulbous. But well, no one's features were perfect, were they? While his face wasn't one that one would encounter on classical statues, it was interesting to look at.

Who was he? Why was he here?

He'd said he wanted to teach, here, to take the position Miss Hilversham had announced in an advertisement. After Miss Brown had resigned as Latin, history and drawing teacher, she had left a gap behind that was not easily filled. Miss Hilversham was a very exacting employer and would not hire anyone. She'd sent away applicant after applicant with a sigh.

"Frances, it is hopeless. They all say they are capable of teaching, but really, they aren't. The last one did not even know when William the Conqueror landed in England, yet she wanted to teach history. Or the one who came yesterday was half colour blind, yet she insisted on being a most excellent instructor of drawing. And I will decline the rest, for none of them have ever taught children." She threw down a pile of letters on her desk with a huff. Soon after, she'd left for Scotland.

No other applications had come in. Until now.

Frances had gone through some trouble taking off the man's jacket. She marvelled at the cut and the fine material. "Weston," she muttered. Wasn't that a rather expensive tailor in London? Frances knew little of these things, and she'd never set foot in London herself. She only knew from her brother that being clothed properly was apparently the most important thing for a gentleman.

Everyone has a Weston coat, Francie, he'd written. *One fairly stands out like a goose in a crowd of swans if one doesn't sport a Weston coat. Can you lend me the funds for one? If not, I will try to obtain a second-hand one, which won't be quite the thing...*

Of course, Frances had sent him the money. She'd also sent him money for boots. For a fellow needed a proper pair of boots to wear if he wanted to call himself a gentleman, Nat said. Hoby's was preferred.

Frances had also pulled off the man's top boots, which she assumed were of excellent cut as well. She wondered whether they were the kind her brother had wanted.

Frances had gone through the pockets in his waistcoat and found several coins, a golden watch, and a silken handkerchief with the initial H on it.

She frowned. He was most definitely a gentleman. Whether he indeed was well educated and capable of teaching a group of girls in Latin, history and drawing was an entirely different matter altogether.

He stirred in his sleep.

Frances would return to her own room and get some sleep. It was well past midnight.

Outside, it was still snowing.

CHAPTER 4

*I*t was the silence that awoke him.

That, and the ticking of the clock, which he found oddly soothing.

There'd been a clock just like that back in Heshwig Hall.

He opened his eyes and stared at a whitewashed ceiling. A chandelier hung from it, nothing too elaborate, and dark green velvet curtains hung by the windows.

He squinted against the brightness outside. He blinked in disorientation and passed his hand over his eyes.

It was snowing so hard outside that it formed a white sheet that hung from the skies.

This was an unfamiliar room. He was lying on a sofa, not his bed, covered by a blanket, and under his head was a down pillow. He pulled himself up to his elbows. Someone had pushed two armchairs next to him, like one would to keep a child from toppling down on the ground. On the table next to him stood a cup of cold tea, a glass of water, a bowl, and a wet washcloth.

His shirt felt damp, and his head thrummed. His mouth was dry. Percy reached out for the water glass and drank in thirsty gulps.

This cleared his mind somewhat. Where the deuce was he?

This wasn't Heshwig Hall, like he'd at first thought. Neither was it any of his friends' hunting lodges. He'd never been in this room before.

He pulled himself up, dragged his hand through his hair once, twice, and got up. He felt wobbly on his feet. He looked around for The Necessary. Someone had left one discreetly behind a screen, a porcelain device with a lid on.

Afterwards, he looked around.

Again, the silence.

Stepping out gingerly into the hallway, he expected to encounter a maid or a footman, but there was no one.

Had the entire world come to a standstill?

Only the clock ticked, and snow fell outside, silently.

He walked along the hallway; it smelled of wood polish and beeswax, and something else.

Paper, maybe. Chalk?

He peeked into an open door.

There were tables and long benches, and a blackboard. A pile of books.

Ah. The memories rushed back.

He was at that school. In Bath.

He'd come here to apply for a position as a teacher.

And there'd been someone else.

A gentle, sweet person who'd appeared like an angel.

Just at that moment, a sweet, ethereal tune sounded through the hallway.

Angelic tunes, definitely, he thought, as he followed the tune.

He must be still dreaming.

FRANCES WAS IN THE COMMON ROOM AND STARED AT THE holly and the mistletoe on the table. The children had gathered the greens in the forest and parks and returned with far more than was needed. They also normally decorated the entire house with it. But now that everyone had left precipitously, the house was still bare of any decoration, and it was almost Christmas eve. It would be up to her to hang up the greenery. But was there any point to it?

Christmas used to be an important event in her parents' home when she was little. It had been such a loud, cheerful affair. No matter how tight his purse strings were, her father always managed to obtain a Christmas goose, and her mother had made Christmas pudding. They'd stuffed their bellies with the sugar plums and ginger nuts that the Squire's wife handed out. They'd gone wassailing and played games all night... Until that Christmas day when her father had pulled on his coat and announced he'd pick up the Christmas goose from the farmer. He turned at the door with a little smile, told her he loved her, and left.

Frances stared at the holly in front of her with blind eyes.

Her hands moved as if of their own volition. She twisted the holly to a circle, fastening it with wire. She wrapped around some ivy as well and considered adding in some rose hip. Working with her hands was soothing. She always hummed or sang quietly to herself when she worked, even when she corrected student papers. Sometimes it was a tuneless melody, at others she chose a song. Deeply engrossed in her work, Frances sang *The Holly and the Ivy*. Humming at first, then quietly singing, then somewhat louder. No one was hearing her anyhow, and she enjoyed the echo of her voice in the place. She could sing to her heart's content. After that, she sang *Greensleeves*. Frances had a clear, sweet voice that rang out brightly.

She finished binding the wreath on the long clear finale.

"That was amazing," a voice said behind her.

She dropped the wreath and whirled around with a suppressed shriek.

He leaned against the door frame, with a look of delight on his face. "I haven't heard anyone sing so beautifully since," he shook his head, "I can't remember. I don't think I've ever heard such a lovely voice before."

Frances snapped her mouth shut and placed her hands on her hips. "Why are you up? You should be resting."

"I heard an angel sing, and I followed the voice." He stepped into the room. He supported himself on the wall, as he still seemed somewhat shaky. Goodness, he was tall. She had to tilt her head back to look into his face. Despite his size, he looked like a boy who'd just tumbled out of bed, which he did, of course, with his tousled blond hair and his shirt hanging out of his trousers. He stood in stockinged feet in front of her, a look of admiration on his face.

Frances felt a flush creep over her neck and looked away.

"Forgive me for intruding on you like that. I woke up and did not know where I was. Then I heard your voice and followed it. This is the seminary in Bath, isn't it? How long have I been ill?"

Frances picked up the wreath from the floor and set it down on the table. "Nearly three days. And yes, this is the seminary."

"Three days! Good heavens." A look of consternation crossed his face. "I have been prostrate for three days?"

"Yes. It is Christmas eve. How are you feeling?"

He was still pale, but there was decidedly more life in him than had been in the previous days.

"My knees still feel somewhat wobbly, and my head throbs, but otherwise, I am fine. The fever is gone."

"Do sit down. If you topple over again, you will have to sleep on the floor in front of the fireplace here, because I will not be able to summon the strength to drag you back to the drawing room."

He took her advice and sat down in a chair. "Three days! Christmas eve!" He looked disconcerted. "I must apologise for having encumbered you so. Is that what you've had to do? Drag me on your own?"

"You regained consciousness for one moment and obliged me by getting up and sitting down on the sofa."

"I am not usually in the habit of fainting." He looked about. "Was there no one around to help you? Should this place not be full of the sounds of children, students and other people?"

Frances untied the apron she was wearing and folded it. "The students have already left for their holidays. The teachers as well, and the headmistress, as I have already told you, but you may not have registered that since you were feverish, is not here. To make things worse, it has snowed heavily the last three days and the streets are closed. We are fairly snowed in."

Frances had caught Martha earlier this morning, gaunt and feverish, as she attempted to clear out the soot in the drawing room's fireplace, but Frances had shooed her back to her room with the strict order to remain there until she was fully recovered. Mrs Beedle, the cook, had not returned yet, and she'd received no missives with instructions from Miss Hilversham. No doubt the postal system had collapsed in this weather, and Frances was getting worried. The storage room was well stocked, however, to last well over Christmas. But to be all alone with a stranger, an ill man to boot, was not Frances's idea of Christmas.

Her worry must have shown on her face.

"A dire situation indeed. And I have not contributed, I see. I apologise for having been such an inconvenience. Did we introduce each other? I can hardly remember." He jumped up again, pulled down his shirt, and bowed crookedly. "Percy Tiverton at your service."

Frances suppressed a smile. In his stockinged feet and shirtsleeves, bent in a half-crooked bow, he looked somewhat comical.

"Frances Littleworth," she replied, and made a quick curtsy.

"Frances Littleworth," he echoed. "And who are you, Frances Littleworth?" It was clear he could not place her. Was she a servant? A maid? She wore an old blue woollen gown, which was warm but certainly out of fashion.

"I am teaching here and currently representing the headmistress."

His face brightened. "Let me guess. You teach music."

She inclined her head.

"You have not filled the position of a Latin, history and drawing teacher, have you? Because I would be very interested in applying for it."

"Yes, so you have said."

"I have come for an interview," he began, then stopped. He looked down at himself and frowned. He mumbled something and left the drawing room. Frances looked after his retreating figure, somewhat puzzled. Then she shrugged and set about clearing the table, which was still strewn with snippets of greenery. She was rolling up the red ribbon when she heard him clear his voice behind her.

"If I may. My name is Percy Tiverton." He was wearing his coat, had pulled on his boots, and had clearly attempted to comb his hair with his fingers. His cravat was haphazardly tied.

"I know. We have just been introduced." Frances chuckled.

"Indeed, but not formally. Not properly, as one is wont to do when one applies for a position, you see."

"Is this to be an interview, then?" She gestured at the chair opposite her. "Very well. Have a seat, sir."

"Thank you."

"So, Mr Tiverton. This school indeed direly needs a Latin, history and drawing teacher. What makes you think you are suitable for this position?"

"The advertisement says," his hand went to his breast pocket searching for the piece of paper, then to his trouser pockets, "confound it, I seem to have lost the paper. Never mind. I recall the words precisely. You are looking for a single, respectable, and highly educated person who can take this position. I fulfil all requirements. I am single, respectable, and I have been educated in Cambridge."

Cambridge was good. Nat was up in Cambridge as well. "What did you study?"

"Law."

"Law! Not history or Latin?"

"My father deemed it appropriate for me."

"You studied law because your father wanted you to?"

He shifted uncomfortably in his chair. "I will be honest. I admit I discovered fairly early on that it did not suit me, so I did not complete those studies. But that is of no consequence, as I have studied both Latin and history with my tutors since I was a child. I've also read the *History of England.*"

Frances looked sceptical. "Just because you have studied both subjects does not mean you can teach them."

"I beg to disagree. *Amor vincit omnia.* Vergil."

Frances raised an eyebrow. "I doubt Miss Hilversham would be impressed by this. Love conquers all? Really?"

He thought. "*Ut ameris, amabilis esto.*"

"Ovid. If you want to be loved, be lovable. Try again, Mr Tiverton."

"*Amore et melle et felle fecundissimus est.*"

Frances burst into a peal of laughter. "Love is rich with both honey and venom."

He threw up his hands. "How confounding! I seem to be capable of only coming up with phrases pertaining to love."

"Are you in love, maybe?" Frances bit down a smile. She did not know that there was an adorable dimple in her cheek when she did that.

He blinked at her.

She looked away. "Never mind. Forget I asked that. Next. History." She cleared her throat. "When did William the Conqueror land in England?"

"Seriously?"

"Seriously. More than one applicant was unable to answer this very basic question."

"Behold me astonished. William the Conqueror landed in-uh. Ten-uh-uh."

Frances tapped a pale fingernail on the table. "Well, Mr Tiverton?"

He scrunched up his face.

Once more, Frances had the irresistible urge to laugh. She pulled her mouth into a severe line. This was serious business. She was interviewing a future teacher. Miss Hilversham was most exacting and would not hire anyone.

He snapped his fingers. "Ten sixty. Am I correct?"

Frances rubbed her eyebrow.

"I was only funning. It was ten sixty-five. Sixty-six I mean. I would put my bet on sixty-six."

Frances's fingers drummed again on the table. "Mr Tiverton, this is no joking matter."

"No, it is terribly serious." He cleared his throat. "Of course it was ten-sixty-six. Every child knows that. I am sorry. I couldn't help but tease you a little. You are so adorably teasable when you glare at me like that." His eyes twinkled.

She felt a hot flush creep up her cheeks. There was a decidedly flirtatious look in those smiling hazel eyes. Frances would not fall for it. She sat up straight and pursed her lips in disapproval. "Mr Tiverton. May I remind you that this is an interview, and I am the headmistress representative? Treat this situation with the gravity it demands."

"Yes. Of course." He pulled himself up straight. "I was merely trying to convince you I do know history very well. Even though I am rather terrible at remembering numbers." Mr Tiverton pulled his lips into a crooked smile. In response, she frowned even more severely at him. "Arithmetic has never been my forte. Numbers tend to somehow switch positions. But then you are not looking for a mathematician, are you?"

Frances searched for diplomatic words. "No." She took a big breath. "Mr Tiverton."

"I know all about the Romans, however," Mr Tiverton interrupted. "They built wonderful aqueducts, and I can tell you precisely how they did it. I am excellent at reconstructing the seven world wonders. In miniature, I mean. Not in actual size."

"Miniature? How so?"

"Using all sorts of material. I once reconstructed the Colosseum using only tiny sticks. A miniature version. This big." He lifted a hand and showed her thumb and index finger spread apart.

"Very well. So you are rather creative and are in possession of some handicraft skills. But regarding your teaching qualifications. Do you have previous experiences? References?"

"Previous experience. Yes. Certainly. I have taught, er, er, one may say it was teaching, though not actually in a classroom, not in the sense as is commonly understood; however, I have certainly had such experience." He scrunched up his face as he thought.

Frances noticed his eyes lit up when he smiled, and

darkened when he was thoughtful, like now. She really ought not to notice things like that. "Yes?"

He cleared his throat. "Yes."

"References?"

He searched his pockets. "Confound it. Haven't I had a letter somewhere? I have lost all my belongings."

Frances shut her eyes for a fraction of a second. "That may have been my fault. You must forgive me. When you fainted, I searched your pockets to find any kind of identification. There was a watch and several coins, which I placed on the table in the drawing room. Then there was your trunk, which I left outside in the hall. There was no letter in any of your pockets. Maybe you have left them in your trunk."

She'd been sorely tempted to rifle through his trunk, but she'd thought that would have been a step too far.

"Oh, I see."

"Mr Tiverton." She decided to be frank. "You have never taught before."

He looked at her ruefully. "I am afraid I have not."

"Neither do you have any references."

His shoulders slumped.

"I am very sorry, sir. But I cannot, in good conscience, hire someone who has neither experience nor references. This is one of the best seminaries in England, and we have a reputation to uphold. Our students are from well-to-do families who expect only the best. Miss Hilversham would never tolerate having a teacher who is not outstanding in his profession."

He tilted his head aside as he contemplated her words thoughtfully. Then he gave her a sudden smile, and her heart jumped inexplicably. "The best of the best? Behold, you are looking at him."

"Excuse me, but how old are you?" Frances burst out.

"Twenty-six. Is that it? Am I too young?" He was two years younger than her. Frances shook her head. "No. It is actually of no consequence. Not if you are an excellent teacher. I don't know why I asked. The situation is this." She looked at him openly. "While we need an additional teacher or two, Miss Hilversham is more than exacting about the qualifications. There need to be at least three references. And mind you, she follows up on each one of them. Prospective teachers who have passed the initial interview also need to prove that they can teach by going through a trial teaching session."

"A trial teaching session? What is that? It sounds intimidating."

"You teach a class while she assesses you."

"Not intimidating, but thoroughly terrifying."

Frances lifted her shoulders. "It is as it is. Most applicants fail this second stage."

"It seems I don't even get to this second stage?" He was imploring her to deny it.

Frances stood up. "I am very sorry, Mr Tiverton. I am certain it is best for everyone involved if you seek your employment elsewhere." It came out harsher than she intended.

He slumped in his chair. He suddenly looked tired and defeated. Frances felt a pang, but then steeled her heart. It was better this way. Not only was he unqualified, but there was something about him that told her it was better he was gone. She did not like at all how her pulse increased every time he smiled at her. Then this flirtatious behaviour towards her. It was not the thing. She'd fallen for a man's flirtation once; she would not do so again. To shield herself from it, she wrapped herself tightly into the mantle of the strict headmistress.

"You still look very much exhausted, Mr Tiverton. It may well be you have not entirely recovered from your illness. I can offer you one more night to recover completely from your sickness; however, I must insist that you leave after that." Even one night might be too much, a voice whispered inside her.

He pulled his hand through his hair. "Of course. I have encroached on your hospitality and inconvenienced you in every manner possible. I haven't even thanked you properly, have I?"

"There is no need for thanks."

Suddenly, he looked up. "There is just one more thing. May I have a sheet of paper and a pencil, please?"

"Of course." Frances assumed he wanted to write a letter. She got the writing utensils and placed them in front of him on the table. He took a book as a support, placed the paper on it, and wrote.

In the meantime, Frances cleared the table of the remaining greenery and swept the floor. She looked at the holly wreath and the mistletoe bough thoughtfully. Her initial joy at preparing the decorations had dissipated entirely. There may be no purpose in hanging this up. What for? There would be no celebrations this year. She'd rather not hang it up than find herself all alone under the mistletoe. All this merely reminded her of earlier times that were long gone and would never come again. She placed both into a box to put away later.

"There." He put his pencil down. He squared his shoulders. "Since I lack references, I have decided I need to prove my worth otherwise." He pushed the paper towards her. "Never mind teaching Latin and history. While I believe I could do it, you are right that these are not the subjects I excelled in. I am specifically interested in the position of the drawing master."

Frances picked up the paper and gasped.

"This is only a small sample of what I can do. I can also paint: oil, water, pastels, chalk, you name it. Mosaic, pottery and sculpture. I can work with stone and wood equally well; however, I much prefer wood, because the material is more alive. Murals. Do you want me to paint a mural here? I noticed the wall in the hallway is rather bare, stripped of any wallpaper. We can also turn it into a class or a school project. Miss Littleworth?"

"This is—absolutely—utterly amazing!" Frances had seen nothing like it before. The closest she'd seen was a print of Dürer once, of hands folded together, praying. "It is unbelievably lifelike."

"Well? Do you like it? I can teach your students how to draw like this."

Frances shook her head. "I don't think anyone can really learn how to draw like that. You have been born with a tremendous gift, Mr Tiverton. The rest of us need to be content with much simpler abilities. When I sketch hands—" Frances uttered a sudden laugh, "it is all rather uncoordinated, and the fingers look like sausages. What a beautiful sketch this is. Why do you want to teach? With a patron, you can exhibit your work and gain even some fame, I daresay."

He shrugged. "I don't want fame. And I don't want to work for a patron. Then you have to paint what they want you to paint. Wouldn't even know how to go about getting one. I like the idea of teaching very well. I believe I would be good at it." He bent forward. "I can teach others how to draw like this. Yes, some of it is talent. But most of it is technique. It has to do with seeing, observing." He lifted his hand and turned it in front of his face as he gazed at it. "Seeing, truly seeing what it looks like. What is underneath the skin. The veins. The muscles. The flesh." He was muttering to himself. "You have to be able to see the space between the fingers, too. That what is not material." Frances watched him, fascinated. "And when you draw a person, you have to truly see her." He transferred his gaze to her. "Not just the exterior, but seeing, truly seeing what is beneath." He studied her face with open interest.

Frances squirmed.

"Let me prove it to you. Let me, after the students return, teach a trial class and prove to you I can not only draw, but I am the best drawing teacher this school has ever seen."

Frances could not tear her gaze away from the intensity on his face, the deep passion and joy burning in him. It was as if his entire being had lit up. She felt how he drew her in, an irresistible pull that was fascinating in its seductive sweetness.

She steeled her arms against the tabletop in resistance as she struggled to keep a cool mind. It was so unorthodox. What would Miss Hilversham have done? This complete stranger, who'd collapsed on their doorstep, who'd been ill with fever, whom she'd nursed, listening to his jabbering nonsense in his fever dreams, and who'd insisted he wanted to become a teacher at their school, yet clearly had no qualifications. But goodness, how he could draw. She would be helplessly ensnared in his charm if she wasn't careful. She couldn't, simply couldn't, afford this.

"Mr Tiverton, you have a God-given talent, but that doesn't mean you are a good teacher," she said gently.

"Please give me a chance." He was fairly pleading. "Let me at least try."

It was an echo of what she'd said nearly seven years ago to Miss Hilversham.

Miss Hilversham had also given her a chance when she'd applied four years ago. She'd had no references either, since her previous employer had refused to write her one. She'd been unjustly let go of her position because the son of the house had flirted with her and stolen a kiss. Before she could blink, she'd found herself alone on the street. Luckily, she found a newspaper on a bench, with Miss Hilversham's advertisement in it. She'd spent her last coins on a coach to Bath. The headmistress had listened to her, merely raised an eyebrow, opened a door that led to a classroom full of children, and told her to teach. Oh, how Frances had taught! If there was something she was born to do, it was teaching.

Miss Hilversham had lifted her hand after ten minutes. "That will do," she'd said in that crisp, clear voice of hers. "You are hired."

Her life had changed because someone had believed in her. She had been given a chance. It was only fair that she gave him a chance, too.

Frances looked down at the drawing. "Very well, Mr Tiverton. You deserve this chance. When our students return for the next term, you are to teach them in a trial

class. Mayhap, by then, Miss Hilversham has returned."
And if she did not, she would have to make this decision
on her own.

The smile that broke over his face took her breath
away. His eyes lit up and looked almost golden. He took
her hand and placed a fervent kiss on its back. It zinged
up her arm, through her entire system, and brought a
flush on her face. She pulled her hand away gently.

"You will not regret this. You will hire me. In fact, you
will beg me to stay." His boyish grin was infectious.

"We will see, Mr Tiverton," Frances could not suppress
a smile, even though deep down she wondered whether
she'd made the right decision.

He got up, took some steps towards the door, then
turned, asking, "So, I return the day after Twelfth Night?"

Frances nodded. "That is the day the students return."

She followed him out into the hall, where he found his
coat hanging and pulled it on. "I will need to find accommodation immediately, then." He picked up his trunk,
which was standing in the hallway.

"Oh. You are not from this area?"

He rubbed his neck. "No. I came directly from
Lincolnshire. I have not had the opportunity yet to find
any rooms. I'd already felt unwell in the mail coach, and
barely made it here."

"My offer for you to stay another night here to regain
your strength stands, Mr Tiverton," Frances said as he
opened the front door.

A flurry of snow blew into the house. The wind
howled.

Frances turned away as the icy wind bit into her
cheeks. "Goodness, there's a veritable snowstorm out

there." The path to the street had completely disappeared. It was dark, and the lamps had not been lit yet, probably because the lamplighter had problems fighting his way through the snow. "It has been snowing heavily the past few days. I daresay most of the roads are closed and trans-portation has broken down. It must be the reason Mrs Beedle hasn't returned yet." Frances muttered to herself, frowning. "She said she'd return by Christmas eve."

"Mrs Beedle?"

"The cook."

What should she do? Harbouring a sick man in the house was one thing; a recovered one living in the same house with her over a longer period was an altogether different matter. If word got out that she was staying all alone with a man… On the other hand, he was still pale, and there were dark circles around his eyes. She couldn't send him out there. He'd collapse before he reached the front gate.

Frances chewed on her lower lip thoughtfully. Besides, it was Christmas. One ought to show charity towards one's fellow human being on Christmas.

"Mr Tiverton, I don't think it is a good idea that you go out there. Not in your current state. You will catch your certain death, and I am in no mood to drag your corpse through the snow."

"It is not ideal," he agreed. "It might raise all sorts of questions if one is seen dragging a corpse through the snow. What might the neighbours think? Come to think of it, what will they think if they find me staying here, not as a corpse?" Again, that flirtatious twinkle in his eyes.

Frances pressed her lips together primly and firmly shut the door. "Oh, never mind the neighbours. Let them think what they want." She led him back to the reception room. "We will do things as follows. You move in right away to the new teacher's room. I will ask Mrs Benningfield, who is not only our sponsor but also a good friend, to send us a maid until Martha is well again. Until classes resume and you have the chance to prove your mettle, you may make yourself useful about the school, getting yourself acquainted with the place, and preparing yourself for your job. There are some little repairs that need to be done about the house. I recall you saying that you are good at working with your hands?"

"Indeed." He flexed his long fingers. "My hands are at your service."

"There is one condition, however." A steep frown appeared on her forehead.

"I am all ears, Miss Littleworth."

"The condition is that... that..." She flushed and looked away.

He raised one eyebrow, then the other. "Yes?"

This shouldn't be so difficult to say. She took a big breath. "The condition is that your conduct is to be entirely as a professional teacher, entirely collegial toward me and respecting the position I represent. No jokes. No s-seductive flirtations." Her head was glowing crimson.

His eyes widened. He opened his mouth, then snapped it shut again. He was evidently speechless. Then he caught himself. "Certainly. Absolutely. Unequivocally."

"Unequivocally no? Or yes?"

"No."

"No?"

"Yes."

"No? Yes?" She knit her forehead together. "Mr Tiverton, are you in agreement with me, or not?"

"I said so, didn't I? Though I must say, in defence of your most unexpected and most execrable shredding of my hapless personality: I usually tend not to go about flirtatiously seducing, or was it seducing flirtatiously?—whatever manner of seduction it is you fear—hapless women, especially those who are to be my working colleagues. It isn't quite the thing to do, is it? Especially when one has just met."

Could her cheeks glow any more red? They felt like they were about to burst into flames. Again, there was that twinkling look in his eyes, and something else, something that disturbed her even more. It was a devilish gleam. Most definitely.

"No, it isn't the thing to do at all," she replied severely.

He regarded her thoughtfully. "Truthfully, it never would have occurred to me. Although now that you have put the notion in my mind..."

"Mr Tiverton!"

"Miss Littleworth!"

They stood staring at each other. Frances was determined to throw him out on the spot if his next words were the wrong ones. "Pray cease joking. This is no joking matter."

"No, it is not. I apologise. I didn't mean to tease you. But as I said before, you seem irresistibly teas—Never mind, never mind. I do want this position. I am determined to be on my very best behaviour. It would never occur to me to take advantage of a woman. Least of all one who is to be my very revered superior. Please do not worry. You may trust in me. I will put in every effort to be the professional colleague you seek." He seemed sincere.

Frances exhaled. "I certainly hope so, Mr Tiverton."

"You must excuse my propensity to joke. It is no doubt a character flaw of mine, however entirely harmless. It comes from the fact that I feel overwhelmingly relieved that I have found a position. In fact, I feel so relieved I am about to perform a Scotch reel on the carpet. My grand-mother was Scottish, you see. No need to look so alarmed! I shall pull myself together and walk up those stairs in a stiff and proper manner. Even though it is Christmas eve. And you have just asked me to stay over Christmastide. Is this not a reason to make merry? However, given the horrified expression on your face, which is entirely understandable, Christmas or not, snowstorm or not, I shall refrain from exhibiting any, er, inappropriate behaviour."

"Mr Tiverton." Frances grasped her head. "What is the point of your ramble?"

He cleared his throat. "My point being: I will only stay if you are certain you want me to." He emphasised the 'certain.'

"Yes," Frances replied quietly. "Do stay. It won't be such a lonely Christmas, then."

His face broke out into a smile for the second time of the day, making Frances feel all dizzy.

He bowed.

"It will be a pleasure."

CHAPTER 5

*N*ever in his life had he felt so light.

It was excessively odd, for never in his life had he been forced to survive without his valet, his butler, a host of footmen and other servants who catered to his every need.

Miss Littleworth had shown him a room on the upper floor, facing a snowy garden. It was furnished with a simple bed, a wardrobe, a commode with a bowl and pitcher, and a fireplace.

"It faces South, so you will have sufficient light for working during the day." She set down a candle on the mantle. "You'll have to make your own fire because our housemaid is still indisposed."

It had taken him a while to get a good fire roaring, but he'd done it. He'd also unpacked his trunk, folded his clothes into the commode, and aired his own bed. His valet would have been proud of him. He felt proud of himself, too, like he'd accomplished something monumental.

He saw the housemaid on his way down the stairs, attempting to clear out soot from the fireplace in one of the classrooms. Miss Littleworth had scolded her so soundly it had echoed in the entire school.

"You will not set foot outside of your room until you are completely healthy. I will not, I repeat, will not have you up and about when you are ill."

"But Miss, it's Christmas tomorrow," she'd said in between coughs. Her voice had sounded raspy and breathless. Miss Littleworth would have none of it, however, and she'd returned to her room.

Frances Littleworth. Frances. The name suited her. She was little in every respect, dainty like a doll. She barely reached his shoulder and had to lift her head to meet his eyes. The tip of her nose was dusted ever so lightly with freckles. Like fairy dust. There was a sweetness about her that made him want to gather her up in his arms and protect her. Yet she'd made it clear on more than one occasion that her appearance belied the personality behind it. Oh! She could be fierce. There was a steeliness that she'd wrapped around herself like a mantle. Every time he attempted a flirtation, she pursed her lips and pulled the mantle a little tighter. He had to admit, it egged him on, prompted him to tease a little more, just to see how far he could go, whether she would drop her facade, whether he could make her smile.

He'd merely managed to make her cross and utter that utterly cryptic remark that had left him gob smacked. He felt affronted. Flirtatiously seduce hapless women? Who did she think he was?

Yes, he liked to joke and flirt; it meant nothing. However, to imply that his behaviour towards women was intentionally seductive filled him with outrage. The problem, of course, was that he'd proven her correct by joking even more, to cover his fury.

It was clear she did not trust him. Yet she'd given him a chance. She hadn't thrown him out. For that, he'd be eternally grateful.

He'd tried to capture her face in a pencil sketch earlier but ended up crumpling the paper and throwing it into a corner. The floor was littered with paper balls; sketches that did not satisfy him, that he considered failures. The light from the fireplace wasn't sufficient. He'd have to try again tomorrow.

He wanted to capture that air of hers, the sweet, gentle innocence of her bearing. The slightly suppressed smile, the joy that was radiating from within, but laced with a sense of melancholy. He'd seen that expression only once, in a painting of the Madonna of the Meadows by Raphael, which he'd admired in Vienna on his travels to the Continent.

That same serenity. That same half-smile.

He wanted to draw it.

There was something else she'd said that made him thoughtful. He assumed she'd given him this chance out of the goodness of her heart, because he'd been sick and too weak to struggle his way through the snowdrifts outside, not knowing where to go, where to get accommodation. He was a stranger in this town, and he had not thought to reserve a room elsewhere.

It wasn't only altruism, however.

He believed, no, he hoped, it was also because maybe, just maybe, his company over Christmas meant something to her.

"It won't be such a lonely Christmas, then," she'd said, lightly, almost jokingly. But there'd been a serious note underneath.

Yet she hadn't hung up the greenery, as was customary on Christmas eve.

She'd played around with it when he entered, but then placed it all in a box and set it aside.

He wondered why.

THE NEXT MORNING, HE WENT DOWN TO THE DINING ROOM and found a note on the table.

It has stopped snowing, and I have decided to go to Christmas Mass. Please help yourself to your breakfast. Frances Littleworth.

A simple breakfast was laid out for him. Toast and jam, and a pot with tepid tea.

He looked outside the window as he ate. Indeed, the snow had stopped, and the garden and trees were padded with a thick layer of snow. The sun had come out, and it glistened. Percy felt a pang of regret. He would have enjoyed accompanying Miss Littleworth to church, but he realised it might have still been a feat somewhat beyond his physical ability. He could see that someone had shovelled a small corridor of snow along the street where one could walk. It would be cumbersome if it were a long walk. The bigger streets were cleared already, and more than one sleigh had passed by.

What would he do while she was gone?

His eyes fell on the box with the greenery.

CHAPTER 6

*I*t was good that Mr Tiverton hadn't gone to church, Frances told herself, as she trudged through the snow. It was Christmas morning. Her boots were caked with snow, and her toes were freezing, even though she'd pulled over two pairs of woollen socks. The weather was bright, and the sun finally shone; however, it was crackling cold, and she was chilled to the bone. Church was at the bottom of the hill where they lived, and she'd heard the bells from afar. Mr Tiverton would never have made it this far.

She'd sat in the pew, shivering, for it was cold in the church, even though they were huddled closely together, listening to the parson preach his sermon.

The way home would be even more cumbersome, since it was uphill, and her thin boots slid on the snow and ice.

"Miss Littleworth!" a voice rang out.

Frances turned to face a stately woman wrapped in a thick fur coat who was about to enter her sleigh.

"Mrs Benningfield. I wish you a merry Christmas."

"A merry Christmas to you, too, Miss Littleworth. However, I am surprised to see you here. I thought the school was closed because of the measles, with Miss Hilversham gone, too? I thought you left with her for Scotland. Don't tell me you have been all alone in the schoolhouse all this time?"

"Indeed. Although I must rectify a misunderstanding: it was not the measles. I don't know how that pernicious rumour has taken hold. It led to our parents withdrawing their children in panic; however, it was a nasty influenza that our maid Martha succumbed to, not the measles."

"Not the measles, you say? Well, that is a blessing. But what are you saying? You're all alone in that house, with an ill maid?" Mrs Benningfield tsked. "Now, that won't do. I will send you Anna. She's a good, hard-working girl."

Frances grabbed her hands. "I am so grateful. Indeed, I wanted to ask you for some support. But you always know what we need before we even have the chance to utter the word!"

Mrs Benningfield looked at her benignly. "It is a pleasure, my dear. You know how much I enjoy supporting the teachers. But we will talk later. I must go, there is so much to do. Do join us tonight for Christmas dinner? It would be a pleasure to have you, and you should not be on your own over Christmas."

A spark of joy flushed through Frances. "I am truly grateful for this invitation. However, I really have to stay at school, for Mrs Beedle might return any moment, and there's Martha to tend to as well. Besides, Miss Hilversham has given me responsibility over the school, and I take this very seriously. I dare not leave longer than it took for me to go to church. Also, I am not entirely alone. We have a new teacher, and he's fallen ill, too. So you see, my hands are full."

"Miss Littleworth, I seem to have heard that you say your new teacher is a 'he'. I may have misheard. Be that as may. I see you are as practical, reliable, and obstinate as always. Miss Hilversham has found a gem in you. I will send you a basket with foodstuff with Anna, for we need to make sure you are fed, especially if Mrs Beedle is not here. Can I count on you to join us for our Christmas ball at the Manor? You may bring that new colleague. Especially if he is a 'he'." Mrs Benningfield raised an eyebrow.

Frances flushed. "It would be a pleasure, Mrs Benningfield."

Mrs Benningfield gave her a ride back in her sleigh, dropping off Frances right in front of the stately school-house with the Palladian facade.

Frances closed the iron gate with a creak and looked about at the glistening garden. It was a fairytale landscape. The branches of the beech tree in front of the house were encrusted with a thick layer of white snow.

She entered the house and immediately pulled off her soggy boots. A heady smell of mulled cider, oranges, and cinnamon greeted her. Mrs Beedle must've returned, finally! She entered the dining room and gasped.

The table was fully set, with an unexpected assortment of food in the best china. Next to plates of gingerbread, shortbread, and mince pies were bowls of pea soup, and punch, as well as, oddly enough, a plate full of charred potatoes and chopped carrots. In the middle of the table stood the yule candle, which was lit.

These unexpectedly delicious smells and sights

brought up memories of home. Of a time when every-thing was whole, when the world was bright and when dreams could still come true.

"Martha? Mrs Beedle?" Frances dried the corner of her eyes with her sleeve.

The door opened, and not Martha, but Mr Tiverton entered, with an apron tied over his hips. He had a woebegone expression on his face. "Miss Littleworth! I have terrible news."

"What happened?" He still looked pale from his illness, but the look of stark despair shot a pang of alarm through her.

He hung his head. "I have drowned the Christmas pudding."

It took her a moment to register what he'd said. "You have done—what?"

"Drowned the Christmas pudding. Look." He returned to the kitchen with Frances in tow.

On the iron stove, in a tremendous copper pot, in bubbly, boiling water that sloshed over onto the stove, bobbed a mass of brown something.

Frances stared down at it, blankly. "You have indeed drowned the Christmas pudding. What a feat!"

He lifted a wooden spoon in defence. "I am no cook, but I thought, well, Miss Littleworth is at church, and no one is preparing Christmas lunch. With the cook gone and the maid sick and tralala. And I'd rather not have tepid tea and cold toast for Christmas lunch, if you under-stand. So, what is one to do? I might as well give it a hand. How difficult can it be to warm up food? And as you can see, I managed to boil the potatoes. They turned out somewhat blacker than they ought to look like, but I figured one can peel them and eat them with butter and salt. And that soup from yesterday warmed up nicely in that pot over there. Bread, mince pies, biscuits are available a-plenty. Enter the *pièce de résistance*, our good old plum pudding. I found it hanging in the larder. Heureka, I thought, Christmas is not complete without a plum pudding, is it? So I thought, I could get it warmed up as well." He poked a ladle into the pot and a piece of black pudding swam to the surface. "It's a sad old thing that fell into a thousand pieces. It looks like we're having Christmas pudding soup." He scratched his head with the stick of the soup ladle. "I figure that's better than no Christmas pudding at all, though. Miss Littleworth?"

Frances stared at him, dumbfounded, for a moment, then broke into a peal of laughter. She laughed, bending over until tears streamed down her face and her side ached.

"So you thought, take the cloth off and dump the pudding into the pot like that?"

"I made sure to stir it, too, hard, so it doesn't end up sticking to the bottom of the pot and charred like the potatoes. Isn't that how it's done?"

Frances sat down in a chair, holding her side. "No. That is not how it's done." She wiped her face.

"But it needs to be boiled. I am certain of that. I used to watch our cook do it when I was little."

"It has to be tied up tightly in the cloth. Or else in a pudding basin. For several hours." Frances laughed again.

"Well." Percy scratched his head. "I thought one had to unwrap it first. Who would've known? I'd better stick to my drawing, had I not? What to do with this pudding soup?"

"Let us salvage what is salvageable." Frances took a ladle and fished out the bits and pieces of the pudding. A substantial part of it was still intact, so she pressed it back into a pudding form.

"With some luck we can turn it out, and it won't fall apart." She placed a plate on it and turned it and carefully removed the form. The pudding came out, with a part remaining stuck in the form, and she scraped it out with a spoon and pressed it back into shape. "There. It's a little lopsided, but it'll do. Let us add some holly and pretend it's as good as new."

"Wait. There is something essential missing." Percy picked up the brandy decanter.

"Ah, yes."

He poured a good portion of the brandy over the pudding, possibly more than was necessary.

"And now. We set it on fire, yes?" There was such boyish eagerness in his eyes that Frances had to bite back a smile. "It's not a proper Christmas pudding unless it burns."

"Please do, Mr Tiverton. After having drowned the plum pudding, you might as well burn it. It is all yours."

"I will do it, now." He brought a burning candle to the pudding, and a blue flame engulfed it. Frances could not tear her eyes from his face. He looked so ridiculously, boyishly happy that she had to quench an impulse to press a kiss on his smiling lips.

She recoiled. Good heavens, Frances! What on earth are you thinking?

"Look what we did. It looks wonderful, doesn't it?" He looked so very proud of this accomplishment.

She jolted herself back to reality. "Yes. Yes, it does."

"I am certain it will taste just as wonderful. Shall we, Miss Littleworth?"

She nodded mechanically. He went ahead to the dining room, carrying the *pièce de résistance* on a silver tray.

He placed the plum pudding in the middle of the table and beamed at her. "Merry Christmas, Miss Littleworth."

"Merry Christmas, Mr Tiverton."

Then they ate drowned plum pudding, charred potatoes, half-raw carrots and cold pea soup and drank punch as if there was no tomorrow.

"How thoughtful of Martha to get up early in the morning and decorate the place." Frances shoved the plate with plum pudding aside.

"Yes. Very thoughtful of Martha." He continued to eat quietly, thoroughly pleased with himself.

Something must've shown on his face, for Frances narrowed her eyes. "Mr Tiverton."

"Miss Littleworth."

"You did this." It sounded like an accusation.

He looked at her with wide-eyed innocence. "Pray, what do you mean?"

She lifted a hand. "You decorated this." She pointed at the holly wreath that hung over the fireplace, and a bough of mistletoe that hung over the doorway.

He took a sip of his punch. "Me? Certainly not. It must have been some Christmas sprite."

Frances played with her own glass. "How did you celebrate Christmas with your family?"

How to answer that? It had always been a doleful affair at his home. The Christmas dinners had been too formal, too heavy, with his father sitting on one end of the table, his mother at the other, and himself somewhere in between, seeing neither of his parents because the massive silver candelabras blocked the view. The servants prepared the Christmas decoration, the holly and the ivy. He'd never had anything to do with it. Until today, he'd never, in his life, even touched holly.

"This might sound odd to you, but we have never really celebrated Christmas the way it ought to be celebrated," he eventually said.

Frances leaned her head in her hand. "Mainly obligation and little enjoyment?"

By Jove, she was pretty when she tilted her head like that. That line of her lips. Her finely swung brows. His hands fairly itched to sketch her.

"Precisely," he croaked.

"Why do you think that was?"

"I am not certain. I grew up like this, not knowing it could be different. My father would not have welcomed any kind of celebration of the boisterous, hearty kind. My mother always bowed to his wishes. And I," he shrugged, "spent much of my time at school, later at Cambridge."

"Are you an only child?"

He nodded. "I grew up with a host of elderly aunts and uncles, and great-uncles, and great-great aunts. And did I mention great-grand-cousins-uncles? One doesn't even have names for relations like that. All elderly, old, and ancient. But still breathing, mind you."

Frances choked on a laugh. He loved it when he made her laugh. Her entire being lit up.

"I used to wish for an older brother or sister. They had

to be older," he added. "So I could go fishing with them. Alas, that never happened."

"It sounds like you had a lonely childhood."

"Lonely? Of course not." He said lightly. He used to bribe the servant boys into playing with him, he'd been that lonely. "But how did we end up talking about such a morose subject as my childhood? Tell me about your family, Fran—I mean, Miss Littleworth." Dash it, he'd have to be careful, he was already thinking of her with her given name.

"Christmas used to be the best time of the year when I was a child," she said with some hesitation.

"What happened?"

"My father was a schoolmaster, you see. Our house was always full of people. Students, teachers, neighbours. There were three of us, myself, my brother Nat..." her voice faded, and she shook her head. "My mother loved having a full house. They say she married beneath her station, even though my father was a gentleman and the son of a clergyman. But my mother's family would not recognise him, and so they cut her off."

She pulled her mince pies into little pieces as she talked.

"My mother left her family to be with my father. For love. My father... I remember him as a charming, cheerful kind of man. But he can't have loved us very much after all. He left us on Christmas day. He just walked out and never came back."

Percy pulled a face. "I am sorry. That is beastly behaviour."

"If Mr and Mrs Kent hadn't taken us in, for they were an elderly couple who'd always wanted children, we would have ended up in the workhouse. So you see, Mr Tiverton, Christmas is not all joy and celebration for me at all. I sometimes fear the holiday. It brings up such painful memories."

"Poor little Frances," he said softly. Her childhood had possibly been worse than his.

"Poor little Frances has had to grow up quickly." Her voice hardened. "I became a schoolteacher, and I have supported my family ever since. I am very good at what I do." She glared at him as if he'd challenged her on that point.

He raised his hands in defence. "There is no doubt in my mind whatsoever that you are the most brilliant teacher in this entire school, if not in the kingdom. Let us just say the world. The universe, even?"

"Mr Tiverton!" She glared at him.

"Miss Littleworth!" He grinned back.

She'd pulled on her schoolmistress mantle again. Any minute now, she will waggle her finger at him. That won't do at all.

So, he narrowed his eyes at her. "It would not occur to me in my wildest dreams to challenge you on the notion that you are an excellent teacher. But I insist on challenging you on another notion altogether, and that with full confidence."

"Oh? And that is?" She was cool, collected, and distant. She looked down at him as if she were the queen.

"Cribbage." He leaned back and saw with satisfaction that he'd managed to confuse her. He held back a grin.

"Cribbage?" she echoed, blinking at him. Ah. Did she know she wrinkled her nose when she was confused? Where was his drawing pad?

"Cribbage. I found a cribbage board in one classroom. I daresay you are a hideous cribbage player. Schoolteachers usually are, you see, since they must constantly forbid their pupils from playing the game."

"Oh! That is not true! They are not! On the contrary!"

"Hm. Unless you mean to say teachers confiscate the board so they can play it themselves, in secret? Now, that is an interesting thought." He tipped his finger against his mouth in mock thoughtfulness.

"Mr Tiverton." She pulled herself up haughtily. "You are talking fustian. I will prove to you I am a fine cribbage player indeed. Even though I am a teacher."

"Indeed? That remains to be seen." He leaned forward, "Because I am certain I am better. Shall we bet on it?"

"What would you like to bet on? Money?"

"No." He pretended to think. Then a devilish imp prompted him to say, "a kiss."

Frances jumped out of her chair. "Certainly not! That would be most improper."

"Very well, if you say so. You doubt your ability to win, am I right? Imagine if you lost…. how improper if I were to claim my prize!" He'd never enjoyed himself more when he saw that he'd managed to get her all riled up.

She glared at him. Then, to his great delight, she raised her finger at him and wagged it up and down. "Mr Tiverton. We will play cribbage. I will prove you wrong. I will win. Make no mistake about that. And when I do, you will, as a punishment," she paused, thought a moment, then resumed, "you will, as a punishment, fix the wallpaper in the hallway."

"Deal." They shook hands.

Percy set up the cribbage board in the drawing room.

Frances had taken along the punch bowl and a plate of mince pies. "To fortify ourselves," she explained.

He shuffled and dealt the cards.

Frances hadn't lied. She was indeed a fine cribbage player. In fact, he would have to be careful she did not win. He, in turn, had had so much practice in the clubs in London, he could play cribbage in his sleep. He allowed her to win the first few rounds, then pulled the game to his advantage. He observed closely how a worried crease crept onto her forehead, and how she pulled on her lower lip.

She stared at her last card. Then she threw it down with a sigh. "I see you are about to peg your one-hundred twenty-one points. You are clearly the more experienced player."

"Yes. I said so, didn't I?"

"Mr Tiverton?"

"Miss Littleworth?"

"You are not really going to claim your prize, are you?" Her voice sounded small.

He pretended to think. "I think maybe... I really do think, under these circumstances..." He hesitated, pondered, and weighed his options. Her face turned hopeful.

He shook his face sorrowfully. "I am so very sorry. But I will most definitely have to claim my prize."

"Oh!" She threw down her cards. Before she could get up and rush out of the room, Percy bent over in a flash and planted a firm kiss on those deliciously sweet lips.

"Oh!" she repeated, stunned.

"There, it is over," he was oddly breathless. "And what a prize. I now regret that I didn't go about savouring it more. I could fairly kick myself. Don't throw me that appalled look, it wasn't that bad, was it?"

Frances had fled to the door. "Yes, I mean. No."

"Yes? No? What is it to be, I wonder?"

"You have me all confused." She threw up her hands.

Percy grinned. "Excellent. Take one step back, will you? Just one more. Please?"

Frances looked behind her and saw the mistletoe dangling above her in the doorway.

"Oh. You!" she spluttered.

Percy roared with laughter.

Then someone knocked on the main door.

Flustered, Frances patted her hair and arranged her fichu before she opened the door.

Mrs Benningfield was true to her word and sent her maid Anna with an enormous basket containing a roast goose, another plum pudding, a plate full of mince pies and sweet plums, a loaf full of bread and apples. Anna laid everything out on the table.

Frances stared at the bountiful food. "Goodness! Who is to eat all that?"

"I will." Percy pulled out a chair. "One can never have enough mince pie."

Afterwards, he leaned back in his chair, holding his stomach. "I vow I will not touch another mince pie for the rest of my life. Although," he picked up another one between his fingers and studied the well-formed star on it, "if I had to compare the mince pies of this house to those of the Grand Manor, I must say the ones of this house are far superior."

"Thank you, sir, I try my best," a rusty voice said behind them. A woman wrapped in coat and shawls stood there, with reddened cheeks from the cold, carrying a monstrous basket.

Frances jumped up. "Mrs Beedle! You have finally come."

"I am so very sorry, Miss, so very sorry. I said I would be back by Christmas eve, but I could not, for the life of me, make it across the bridge. The storm and the snow, it was chaos in town, and it was altogether a terrible mess."

"Don't worry, Mrs Beedle. How is your mother?"

"Better, Miss. Thank you so much for having allowed me to visit her. I made sure she's well taken care of, and she'll recover in good time."

"I'm so glad to hear this, Mrs Beedle. This here is Mr Percy Tiverton. He is our newest teacher."

"I am afraid I made somewhat of a mess in the kitchen, Mrs Beedle, in the attempt to cook our Christmas lunch," he said ruefully. "I also ruined our plum pudding."

"Never you mind, sir, I brought another one right here." She patted the basket. "This, and some good, fine roast beef."

"Three plum puddings in a day!" Frances laughed. "We are lucky, indeed."

"I can't eat another crumb," Percy groaned.

"Don't you worry, sir, there are still eleven days of Christmas left." Mrs Beedle disappeared with her basket in the kitchen.

"I will ask Martha to join us," Frances said. "It is Christmas after all, and maybe she feels better today."

Martha did, indeed, feel somewhat better, though pale and with a red nose, and was able to join them to raise glasses of punch. Afterwards, they spent the evening around the fire, sometimes talking, sometimes not.

Frances had been alternately reticent and talkative. As if she sought companionship on one hand, but on the other, for some reason, feared it. He wondered why. Then Percy got up, stretched, and announced it was time to retire.

Later, in his room, Percy thought it was the oddest Christmas he'd ever had. Celebrating with a schoolteacher, a housemaid and a cook. He'd prepared the Christmas meal, played cribbage, and received a kiss. That kiss! He'd intended it to be a playful, harmless kiss. But it had awakened something in him. Something that was stirring in his veins and that was altogether difficult to ignore. Percy tried to push it aside.

But he couldn't get Frances's expression out of his mind, that look on her face when she saw the table. Delight and surprise and something else, like she was choking with emotion. Her expression had been similar when he'd kissed her. Surprise and wonder.

Again, something that stirred in his veins.

Percy pulled out his sketchbook.

Yes, most definitely. It was the oddest, quietest, simplest, and most charming Christmas eve he'd ever experienced. And Frances Littleworth was the sweetest lady he'd ever known.

If only…

If only.

CHAPTER 7

*T*he next day, Frances sat in an armchair by the window in the library and flipped through a book, forcing her mind to concentrate on the words before her. After she'd reread the same paragraph for the fourth time, she shut the book with a huff of impatience. She stared outside the window and saw that it had begun to snow again. She'd come to the library to seek some solitude, which was, if one thought about it, ridiculous, because she was nearly alone in the house.

The truth was that she was hiding from him. She'd heard him walk up and down in his room earlier, then how the stairs creaked as he went downstairs. In the meantime, she'd slipped out of her own room and scurried to the library, shutting the door behind her with a quiet click.

This, of course, was ridiculous.

Why was she hiding from him?

Her thoughts were in a whirl of confusion. Her fingers wandered to her lips.

That kiss! Of course, it had meant nothing at all. A prize he fairly won. It had been a mere peg. It hadn't been a proper kiss, really, she told herself.

Then why could she not stop thinking about it? What had that zinging been that had flashed through her veins? She felt breathless at the mere thought of it.

Disturbed, she flicked the page of the book, only for the sharp edge of the paper to cut into her finger.

"Ow." She sucked on the wound. How can a minor cut like that hurt so much? She stared at the finger and saw how the blood oozed out of the wound.

Ah. Yes. Wasn't she familiar with that question? How could something so insignificant have such disastrous consequences?

How could a harmless flirtation bring about disaster? How could a harmless kiss bring her to near ruination? Had she learned nothing at all from what she'd experienced several years before she joined this school?

That had also been an unexpected kiss, back then, the one that Robert Langley, the son of the house, had given her. He'd rarely been at home, but when he was, he disrupted the entire household.

His favourite pastime had been to flirt with her.

She'd staunchly ignored him, as the governess to his two younger sisters. She'd resisted him, though he was well on his way of weaselling himself into her heart. He'd been irresistible with those snippets of poetry he'd left her, flowers, even chocolates, and many languishing looks.

Then, once, he'd grabbed her in the hallway and stole a kiss from her. She'd gently pushed him back. He'd stammered an apology.

No one had been about; no one had seen it.

Yet someone must have, because the very next day, she found herself on the road, without a home, without a job, without either references or the salary she was owed.

Frances shivered at the memory of how close she'd been to landing in the workhouse. All over a meaningless kiss.

Was she doomed to repeat this foolishness?

For the winter had snowed in a stranger, someone who made her laugh and smile and recapture some of the old Christmas magic that she'd missed for so long. He, too, was a charmingly handsome flirt, just like Robert had been. Yet he was so much more dangerous. For this time, she'd felt herself respond. She'd felt something melt inside her. And what was worse, she'd started to dream and hope again...

It'd been so unexpected that he'd prepared the Christmas feast. Not only that, but he'd also decorated the dining room. He'd done it to please her. And this was what had moved her so.

He'd made her smile and laugh, and he'd teased forth stories of childhood memories that she hadn't discussed with anyone, ever.

After Mrs Beedle had arrived, they'd sat in easy cama-raderie by the fire, sometimes talking, sometimes in silence, drinking punch and eating biscuits, and listening to the crackling of the fire.

She'd felt so comfortable, so at home, so utterly content with him.

Maybe one felt like that when one was married, it crossed through Frances's mind. She shot out of her chair, dropping the leather tome on the floor with a thump.

Good heavens, what on earth was she thinking? She placed her hands on her hot cheeks and shook her head. You have to snap out of this, Frances. This can't be, this won't do. You are the headmistress representative. You can't have these thoughts about a colleague. It wasn't at all proper.

Yes, she'd nursed him, a complete stranger who'd literally snowed into the house. She hadn't even known his name. She was deeply touched when he grasped her hands and called her angel in his fever dreams. She'd sat by his side for hours, not daring to remove her hand, lest he stirred and woke up. She'd got her back in a cramp, and her arm had hurt, but she'd felt oddly content, sitting by him, having the ability to soothe him. When he woke up, it seemed he was aware of her, and he'd begged, "don't leave me," and she'd promised she wouldn't.

But it had been the illness speaking, nothing else.

When he was well, afterwards, he'd shown his true colours, hadn't he?

He was a charmer and a flirt. Just like Robert Langley.

Aside from that, who was he, really? Why was he here? To teach? Really? She hadn't been able to uncover that mystery.

She regretted it deeply that she'd let her guard down and allowed herself to be intimate with someone she barely knew. She would have to work harder at maintaining a professional distance between them.

It would not happen again.

FRANCES WAS SO ENGROSSED IN HER THOUGHTS THAT SHE didn't hear the door open.

He cleared his throat behind her. She whirled around with a gasp, clutching her hand to her heart.

"Here you are. Am I intruding?"

He stood in front of her, bashfully, with that half-crooked smile on his lips, clutching a paper roll in his hands. A blond lock of hair fell over his tall forehead.

Yes, she was about to blurt out. You are intruding. Leave me be before you steal my heart!

She bit on her lip lest those words really escape her.

"I do not want to take up much of your time. It is just —because it is Christmas, you see. I wanted to give you this." He held out a scroll.

She stared at it. "What is it?"

"Take it. It is for you."

Frances took the paper and slowly unrolled it.

It was a pencil sketch of herself, in profile, looking down. So real, so lifelike, yet it was idealised, no doubt, for she was certain she did not look that pretty. Wisps of hair curled over her cheek. She was deeply engrossed in an activity that was not shown on the drawing. A small smile played about her slightly parted lips. Serenity and joy emanated from the painting. He'd seen and captured something in her that she wasn't even aware of herself. Like he'd seen glimpses of her soul. It felt almost invasive.

She gasped. "I don't really look like that."

"Of course you do. Good art roots in seeing, really seeing the object in front of you. I am particularly pleased because I think I caught it."

"Caught what?"

"That particular aura about you."

"Mr Tiverton. I have no idea what you are talking about."

He tilted his head sideways, studying her. "I meant seeing the inner vision I had of you."

The hand in which she held the paper trembled. So did her voice when she said, "We have already established that you are an extremely talented artist." She rolled the paper together and held it out. "But I cannot accept this."

"But why? I made this specifically for you."

Since he did not take the paper roll, she placed it on the table in front of her. She picked up her book.

"I'd rather not be the object of your artistic study. May I ask you to focus on your imminent duties as a teacher and, in the future, refrain from giving me any gifts."

A look of hurt flashed over his face.

She turned away and walked resolutely to the door.

"I don't understand why this would offend you," he called after her. "It is just a gift."

"Mr Tiverton, it is inappropriate for a teacher, one who isn't even officially hired, to give the headmistress gifts. All the time you spent on drawing this would be better invested in preparing your classes. Please take your drawing and refrain from further gifts like this in the future."

She left.

Outside, in the hallway, she drew in a shaky breath. Had she been too harsh? He'd looked truly hurt. She shook her head. It didn't matter. She did the right thing. It was most important that she remained, in all things, professional.

CHAPTER 8

*F*rances hoped to finish her breakfast and disappear to the library again before Percy— that is, Mr Tiverton—appeared. She had begun to think of him with his given name, and that couldn't be. What if she blurted it out one day? Inconceivable. Of course, he had to appear just when she was finishing her porridge. He couldn't have come in ten minutes later, could he?

He bowed rather formally and took his place across from her.

Anna, the maid Mrs Benningfield had sent, served his breakfast.

He stirred in rather a lot of sugar in his tea, Frances noted, as she scraped out the last bits of porridge from her bowl.

The awkward silence between them bothered her. She'd become accustomed to his jokes and smiles, and while she was relieved he'd stopped his flirtations, she felt rather put out at his stiff behaviour.

Well. This is what she wanted, wasn't it?

Since she'd finished her breakfast, she ought to get up and go, but something prompted her to stay.

"What are your plans for today, Mr Tiverton?" She played with her teaspoon.

He looked up fleetingly as he poured some honey over his porridge. "I would like to use the library for some research. With your permission, that is."

"Of course you may use the library. There is no need to ask for permission." She would have to spend her day in Miss Hilversham's office, then.

"I just wanted to make sure that I am not encroaching on your territory, that is all."

"What are you researching?"

"Classical Mythology."

"Ah."

Again, silence fell.

"You will find Homer and Hesiod on the glass-cased shelf at the far side of the library," she offered.

He nodded, then continued eating his porridge in silence.

Frances sighed inwardly. She got up, smoothed down her dress, and stepped to the door. After a moment's hesitation, she turned. "I am sorry if I offended you yesterday. I want you to know I appreciate the kind gesture you made. It was thoughtful of you, despite it being inappropriate."

Thoughtful? Kind? She winced inwardly.

He looked up fleetingly. "You need not worry, Miss Littleworth. It won't happen again. I shall be too busy preparing for classes."

"Very well then," she said stiffly. "I wish you a good day."

She flounced out of the room with a huff.

THIS MR TIVERTON. SHE SHOULDN'T LET HIM NETTLE HER so. She'd done all the right things; it had been appropriate of her to put him into his place. And never mind what he thought of it, and that she'd hurt his feelings. Feelings! This shouldn't be about feelings. They were colleagues. That was all.

Frances drew a hand over her eyes. It was only morning, and she was already tired. She was also spending far too much time thinking about Percy.

She went to the office and immediately saw the stack of letters that Martha had left on the desk.

She picked up the top letter. Nat.

It wasn't always a pleasure receiving letters from her brother. She turned the missive in her hand with growing apprehension, then broke the seal.

PERCY SHOVELLED THE PORRIDGE INTO HIS MOUTH AFTER she left. It was ridiculous that he felt so hurt by her rejection of his drawing. He'd spent almost the entire night up drawing and been so pleased when he'd finally succeeded in capturing her on paper. He thought she'd be pleased.

How wrong he'd been.

Maybe it had been because of that silly kiss? He should never have suggested it.

She was right, and he should focus on his upcoming

classes. He had much work to do. He drank up his tea and pushed the chair back.

Stepping out into the hallway, he paused. What was that?

It sounded like a stifled sob.

It came from the left, the room with the half-open door.

The headmistress's office.

After a moment's hesitation, he walked over and knocked softly on the door. When there was no reply, he pushed the door open.

Miss Littleworth had her head bent on her arms on the desk and sobbed her heart out.

She did not notice he entered. He stood in front of her and cleared his throat helplessly.

"Miss Littleworth... Frances..."

She looked up, her face wet with tears. Strands of brown hair stuck to her temples and around the corner of her mouth. He'd never seen anyone more beautiful.

He crouched next to the desk and peeked up into her face.

"The door was open—" he gestured at the door. "I couldn't help but hear you. Can I be of service?"

She sniffed and rubbed the back of her hand against her nose. "I don't have a handkerchief." Her voice was thick with tears.

"There, there." Percy searched his pockets. Where did he put that blasted handkerchief? He pulled it out from his right breast pocket and handed it to her.

She wiped her face and blew her nose noisily.

"I must look a fright. I am terribly sorry. I just—sometimes it's just too much." She waved a tired hand at the letter in front of her.

"May I ask what is the matter? Not wanting to transgress any boundaries, being the newly appointed teacher here. If the question is too forward, boot me out of the room," he said slightly jokingly.

A shadow of a smile flitted over her face. "It is my brother. He is at Cambridge, where he is supposed to study the common law. Like you did. Sometimes, he goes to London with his cronies. While I am well off here at the seminary, I have to maintain my brother, too. And his lifestyle differs from the kind I lead here. I send him money regularly, most of my income, in fact, to help him complete his studies as fast as possible."

Percy knew where this was leading. He'd known quite a few of those colleagues, who'd happily fritter their fortune away instead of studying. He couldn't quite exclude himself from that, either. Anything was preferable to studying law.

"Let me think. Instead of studying, he spends money on wine, women and song."

"Not entirely. It is more clothes, boots, and gambling."

Percy grimaced. Quite natural behaviour for a young gentleman, in fact, but he'd not tell her in these terms.

"He already spent the entire pouch of money I sent him two weeks ago. Now he is in debt and is asking me for more."

"Scoundrel. What are you going to do about it?"

She pulled at the feathers of her quill. "I am not sure. I feel that no matter what I do, it will not be the right thing. If I send him money, it is not only throwing my hard-earned money down a bottomless pit, but it is teaching him he need not be responsible, for he has a sister who will supply him with endless funds. If I do not send him the money, he will go to the moneylenders, getting himself into a cycle of never-ending debt, interest, more debt, more gambling, more interest, etcetera. I can't sit by and let him ruin his life. He is my little brother, after all." Her lower lip wobbled.

Percy pulled up a chair and sat down. "A difficult situation, indeed. What bothers me about it is that you, as his sister, should not be in this situation to begin with. Is there no guardian? No other family member who you can apply to for help?"

Frances shook her head. "None we are in contact with."

"None you are in contact with," he echoed. "Let me think about the meaning of this. This is basically saying you do have family, but you are not in contact with them."

"It is because," she hesitated and looked at him doubtfully. He returned an encouraging look. Then, as if giving herself an inner push, she spoke. It poured out of her.

"It is because we have family on my mother's side. She was a baron's daughter. I believe there are aunts, and great-aunts, even a peer, in London. Father was a commoner, you see, and that was unacceptable in their eyes. So my parents eloped, and they cut her off. Then my father left—" she swallowed. "I will be forevermore grateful that the Kents opened their house for us. However, then mother passed away from consumption, and Nat and I stayed on with the Kents. They gave us an excellent education, and they wanted Nat to go to Cambridge. They have passed on, too, in the meantime. Smallpox." Frances hung her head. "Nat was clever enough to get admitted into Cambridge on a scholarship. He is a highly intelligent boy. But lately, I don't know why, he seems to be slipping. I think he's fallen into bad company. Clothes, clubs and gambling in London. What's to become of him, of us?" She blew her nose again. "I can't believe I just told you all this. When all you wanted to know was whether we have family elsewhere. In short: yes, we do, but we don't talk."

"I understand. You don't have it easy, Frances. You are a wonderful sister, you know?"

Her eyes teared up again at those words. She pressed the handkerchief against them.

Percy looked thoughtful. "Nonetheless, I believe you should no longer continue on your own in supporting your brother. Not only is he an adult, but he is responsible for his own actions."

Frances nodded. "I know. I know. Should I just sit back and watch him as he ruins himself?"

He folded his arms. "Here is what I think. I think he has come to rely too much on you. His entire life there's been his mother, then the Kents, then you. It is all too easy to ask your sister for money, for what is there to lose, is there? Especially if the sister is a source of endless money supply."

Frances sighed. "You think so? I am afraid you are right. But what else can I do?"

"Write to whatever family is left."

Frances uttered a harsh laugh. "They will not even read my letters."

"Have you tried?"

Silence. "No." She finally admitted. After a moment's hesitation she added, "There is great-aunt Apollonia, whom my mother remembered fondly. They did not write to each other, however. Not as far as I know."

"What is there to lose? If she ignores you, she is confirming that your mother was right in refusing to stay in touch. But if she answers, she might give you the help you need."

"I refuse to go to a family who's rejected us and beg for money." Frances had completely plucked the feathers off her quill.

Percy huffed impatiently. "You're not begging for money. This is about general support. You are asking for help for a brother who is, after all, family. They might actually be glad to support you. As far as I know, that is what family is for. But you won't know unless you swallow your pride and actually ask."

Frances looked at him with enormous eyes. "Do you think so?" she whispered.

He placed his hand on hers. It was small and fluttered like a frightened little bird before it quieted. Percy gave it a gentle squeeze. "I do."

Frances stared down at their hands. She did not pull away. "There is another matter. Mr and Mrs Benningfield have sent us an invitation to their traditional Christmas ball at the Grand Manor House."

"A Christmas ball," he repeated, and looked at her searchingly. Dance with Frances? How would that be?

"Provided you feel quite recovered, of course."

"Oh, these legs should be capable of dancing a jig," he joked.

"The invitation is commonly extended to all the teachers of the house." She made a slight nod. "Which would include you. I thought at first about declining. But then, I thought, why not? Would you like to go?" The diffident expression on her face made her look endearingly young.

"Why not, indeed?" he smiled down into her eyes, and he was rewarded at seeing them lighten up with joy. "It will be a pleasure."

CHAPTER 9

A s he tied his cravat and shrugged into his topcoat, he felt as though he had slipped back into his old skin. His valet, in wise foresight, had packed several formal items of clothing into his trunk, even though he'd protested he'd not need them. He made a mental note to raise the valet's salary when he returned. If he returned, he corrected himself.

Formal dinners, receptions, balls. His life had been defined by that. Normally, he found those events tedious. However, he'd never been asked to a ball by a lady. For her sake, he would go, gladly.

A STEAMING PAIR OF HORSES WITH A SLEIGH WAITED FOR them in front of the school.

"Mrs Benningfield sent them," Frances stepped up behind him. "It isn't far and on a nice, dry day, the distance is easily covered on foot. But in this weather, and at night, it is better to take a conveyance."

She was dressed in a dark blue coat and drew the fur-lined hood over her head. Night had fallen already, and the wind was chilly. She looked wryly down at her shoes.

"I should probably put on my walking boots and change into my dancing shoes at the manor," she mused. "The snow will ruin them, and they're my only pair."

"No matter," Percy said breezily, and swept her into his arms before she could say another word. She weighed less than a child. By the time she'd recovered herself, he placed her gently into the seat of the sleigh and wrapped a fur-lined blanket about her feet. He couldn't help but notice what well-turned ankles she had.

"Thank you. But I am normally capable of walking, one would think." A blush of rose tinted her cheeks. He'd have to capture that colour after they'd returned. It matched the colour of her lips.

Percy turned and nodded at the coachman, who stood behind them. He flicked the reins, and the horses began trotting through the snow.

It was a crystal clear night, the moon and stars were out, the sleigh bells jingled cheerfully and the wind rushed by, brightening their eyes and cheeks. How magical it was.

He was on the way to a ball with a lovely lady by his side; there was the promise of joy and laughter ahead of them, of dancing through the night. The air between them was charged with something delicious, something that he couldn't define, something that caused a tingling in his stomach, a sizzling in his veins.

They did not speak.

He was glad, for it would've killed the magic.

The ride was far too short. A medieval looking mansion appeared, with lights twinkling in its windows, surrounded by a park with white-powdered trees and a frozen lake in front. Upon their arrival, Percy carried her up the stairs and set her off inside in the marbled floor of the vestibule.

"Welcome! Welcome!" Mr and Mrs Benningfield greeted their guests by the door. Mrs Benningfield, dressed in a velvet purple gown with feathers on her turban, took both Frances's hands in hers and shook them heartily. "I am so glad you came."

"This is Mr Percy Tiverton," Frances introduced. "He is our newest teacher at the school."

He bowed.

"Ah. Welcome, Mr Tiverton. Any of our Miss Hilversham's teachers are welcome here." Mr Benningfield led them into the ballroom, which was already packed with people.

It was a cheerful assembly. The entire neighbourhood was gathered, and the people danced with an enthusiasm that took him by surprise. The gentlemen stomped down harder and ladies gripped his hand tighter than he was used to in the genteel ballrooms of London. There were outbursts of laughter and a general atmosphere of merriment. This wasn't just a ball. It was a celebration. The people here danced because they found genuine joy in it. Percy had to think of the balls at Almack's, which were dull, muted affairs where people danced with not even half of the enthusiasm that people had here. The food seemed better here as well, he decided, upon seeing the overladen buffet tables. He'd danced nonstop with the ladies present, and the last dance, a quadrille, had been with Frances.

"Are you enjoying yourself?" she asked as he led her

into a turn. She was light on foot and easy to lead. Her gloved hand in his large one was small and delicate.

"I vow I have never danced so much before. I normally prowl around the buffet, eating."

"Or play cribbage in the card room?" She tilted back her head with an arch look.

"Of course, cribbage." He pretended to think. "But only if the stakes are good." He'd said that on purpose, to see her blush. He watched in fascination as that faint rose spread over her cheeks once more.

She lowered her eyes quickly, her long lashes shadowed her cheeks. Now she was quiet again in her bashfulness. That wouldn't do. He'd have to work at making her feel at ease again.

"However, I find observing people more interesting." Another turn, another twirl.

"Ah yes. The artist's mind is always at work. Are you consistently on the lookout for motifs to paint?"

"Yes. But not only that, I study the composition of colours. Mrs Benningfield's gown, for example. What colour would you call it?"

"Purple."

"Nay. You can do better than that."

Frances laughed. "I can't help it. It looks purple to me."

"Is it more lilac, lavender or mauve? These are all purple shades, wouldn't you agree?"

France's eyes opened. "Oh. I see. Yes, of course. Both lilac and lavender are too light. It is darker, more blueberry-like."

"Mulberry is the word you're looking for."

"Mulberry it is!"

"Describe it to me, as if I were blind." He closed his eyes and promptly stumbled over the next few steps.

Frances supported him with a laugh. "It is difficult. How would one describe mulberry? You do it."

"It is a deep, dark cool plum, not when the fruit is fresh but dried and wrinkled, mixed with a warm wine undertone. Now, find the colours in your watercolour palette. Mix them together. And paint."

"I can see it now. You were right when you said that true art is a matter of seeing."

"This is what I would like to teach, Miss Littleworth. The art of seeing, and then capturing it all with colours on paper."

Frances smiled up at him, and he missed his step again. Her eyes wandered over his shoulder to someone who stood behind him.

"There is a gentleman by the door who's been watching us intently for a while already," Frances told him. "No, don't look. He is still watching us."

"I will take a turn so I can see him."

Percy whirled her in a full turn and saw a tall man with auburn hair stare at them. He clenched his fingers on Frances's waist and pressed his mouth to a firm line.

"Do you see him?"

"Yes."

"And? What do you think?"

"I think he's no one of consequence," he responded lightly. "Let us forget about him and go to the refreshment room. I vow I am half starved."

"After all those mince pies you've eaten?"

"What mince pies? I am certain I can't recall having

eaten any at all. This past... half hour or so." There, he'd made her laugh again. Percy smiled down at her.

After the dance finished, he led her to the adjoining room and brought her a glass of lemonade. Mrs Benningfield's daughter, Mary, stepped up to them and chatted with Frances.

Percy excused himself. With a quick glance, he saw that the auburn-haired man had followed them. Percy stepped into the hallway. The man followed him.

The auburn-haired man accosted him. "So, it is you. I am astonished to find you here."

"Adkins." Percy nodded at him coolly. "I could say the same of you."

"Not so much so. Is my uncle's house after all."

"Mr Benningfield is your uncle?"

"Indeed." Adkins took a glass of champagne from a footman and drank. "Have to visit them once in a while since I'm the heir." He shrugged. "But you? Couldn't believe it when my aunt said you're the new school-teacher? What on earth? Is this a joke? A bet, maybe?"

Percy winced. "Keep this to yourself, will you? I don't want anyone to know I'm here. Not just yet."

Adkins raised an eyebrow. "Now you really have my interest piqued. And the one talking to my cousin Mary? A secret love interest?" He squinted at Frances, who stood by the doorway, talking to Miss Mary.

Percy clenched his fists. "Keep up in this vein, and I'll give you a planter."

Adkins raised both hands in defence. "No need to worry, man. Won't be telling anyone that you're hiding here in a school. Dashedly clever of you, a school! They're all searching for you. Especially your father. Daresay he's sent out the bow street runners."

Percy paled. "The bow street runners?"

"All of London's afoot trying to find you. And here you are, in my uncle's house, dancing with a schoolteacher." He guffawed.

"I'm merely taking some time off."

"Time off. Eh." Adkins wagged his eyebrow and grinned.

"Promise me you will not breathe a word to anyone about it. And leave her out of it."

"Never worry. Shall be silent as a stone. Silent as a tomb. Silent as a—" he searched for another fitting simile.

"Corpse." Percy bared his teeth at him. "For if you aren't, I shall have no scruples at all to turn you into one."

Adkins gave him an injured look. "It would never occur to me to tittle-tattle on my best friends."

"I certainly hope so."

Adkins raised a finger in salutation and strolled off, a knowing grin on his face.

Percy looked after him worriedly.

FRANCES WAS TOO WARM IN HER GOWN. IT WAS A SIMPLE, velvet blue gown, trimmed on the bottom, and she wore a matching velvet band around her neck. She did not know that her neck looked long and white and swanlike in contrast against it, that brown baby curls had escaped from her chignon and framed her face, and that she looked both regal and sweet, both innocent and elegant.

She watched Percy dance with Mary and smiled at how

much he evidently enjoyed himself. Especially when he stumbled over his own feet. He was not too proud to laugh at himself whenever that happened, which was often. He was taller than most men and bent down to his partners to catch what they were saying. When he smiled, the corners of his eyes crinkled. The dance had ended, and he came towards her, with Miss Mary on his arm. They seemed in deep conversation, but as Frances watched them, he looked over Miss Mary's head. Their eyes met, and he winked at her.

"Mr Tiverton has been telling me all about his teaching plans," Mary said. "It makes me want to be a schoolgirl again so I can attend one of his classes."

"Return to school? When you are to be married soon, I have heard?" Frances pulled out her fan, for it was stifling hot in the ballroom.

A big smile formed on her round face. "Indeed! I shall marry my William, finally. We are childhood sweethearts, you know."

"I am so happy for you." Frances felt truly happy for her, but was aware of a slight pang of envy deep down.

"I have always wanted to get married and have a family." Mary took a step forward. Frances stepped back, while Percy leaned against the door frame.

Mary took another step forward. Frances stepped back once more, and a satisfied smile whisked over Mary's face.

"Look!" she pointed upwards. "You two are standing right underneath." Her face was awash with laughter.

Frances looked up. A kissing bough dangled right above them, tied to the frame of the door with a red and green ribbon.

A look of mock horror crossed over Percy's face. "Mistletoe!"

"You must kiss, Mr Tiverton, Miss Littleworth! It is tradition. A kiss and a vow. Well?" She crossed her arms. Several other people who stood by laughed and nudged them on.

"A kiss and a vow? That's new. Normally, it's just a kiss. But a vow? How so?" Percy asked.

"It is a tradition in our house." Mary's eyes twinkled. "You can, of course, choose not to do so, but it will bring all sorts of bad luck down on your heads if you don't."

"You are making this up, Mary," Frances protested.

"Not so. The last couple who refused to kiss had horrible things happen to them."

"Like what?" Percy crossed his arms, laughing.

"The lady lost all her teeth, and the gentleman his hair. They were not yet twenty. Can you imagine? They aged beyond their years before the year was out."

"Oh, the horror! I would never want to lose my hair." Percy tugged at his hair. "My only pride and glory. Miss Tiverton, are you ready?"

"Oh, very well. I must confess, I'd rather keep my teeth." Frances's pulse skittered alarmingly.

Percy lowered his face, his eyes still laughing, but in their depths, there was something that made her catch her breath.

She expected him to kiss her lips, like before, a short, quick, hard peg, but he did not. Instead, he brushed her lips ever so lightly. Like butterfly wings. A delightful shiver ran through her.

"Now, the vow!" Mary's voice reached her through a misty dream.

Percy looked up with a blink. "Vow?"

"Remember, the gentleman must make a mistletoe promise." Mary crossed her arms with an obstinate set to her chin.

"I have one. But it is only for Miss Frances's ears." He placed his hand on her shoulder, bent down, and whispered into her ears.

Her eyes widened. She saw in his that he meant it. Every single word.

She trembled.

Something took hold of her, a familiar dread. Its ice-icy hand clamped itself around her heart and squeezed tightly.

She inhaled a shaky breath. "Mr Tiverton. This is no joking matter."

"It is no joke," he murmured.

She untangled herself from his embrace.

Mary, who'd missed this exchange, clapped. "Well done! You will be held to this promise for eternity."

"Eternity? It is but a mistletoe kiss. No need to make any declarations. This is done, and now we'd better return to school. It is getting late." She strode ahead.

Mary looked after her, a crease on her forehead. "What on earth did you tell her?"

Percy pulled his hand across his neck. The heat in his cheeks had nothing to do with the warmth in the ballroom. "The truth. But it's something she may not be ready to hear yet."

. . .

PERCY WENT AFTER HER. SHE'D PUT ON HER COAT AND pulled the hood over her head. Then she turned to go outside.

"I am sorry if I have overstepped," he went after her. "I did not intend to offend."

"Mr Tiverton, we need to clarify one thing." Frances was out of breath, for she'd fairly run down the stairs to the waiting sleigh.

He lifted both hands. "Don't—"

"This was a lovely ball. It is habitual for the teachers of the seminary to attend this ball. Let us not forget we are to be colleagues here. If either of us value our position at the seminary—regardless of the fact that it isn't at all certain whether you will be hired to begin with as this is a matter that Miss Hilversham will need to decide upon eventually—"

"Wait. Are we back to that again? I thought you were given leeway to hire people," he began.

She shook her head. "This is beside the point."

"What is the point, pray?" He threw up his arms in frustration.

Frances took a big breath. "The point is that we are colleagues. N-not lovers."

"Colleagues. Of course."

She tilted up her chin with determination. "Mr Tiverton. I care for my position here. I'd rather not lose it. It isn't worth it."

He looked like she slapped him. "Not over someone like me, you mean to say."

Frances did not reply, which he took as an affirmative.

. . .

THEY RODE BACK IN SILENCE. GONE WAS THE enchantment. The sense of ease between them.

They were back at the school, which seemed big, dark, empty and cold. He held the door open to her, and as she stepped past him to go inside, he grabbed her hand and bowed over it, as if about to kiss it, but refrained.

"Frances. I meant the promise I made under the mistletoe. Every single word. It was no jest. I am well aware of the proprieties. You need not fear. I will not be a risk to you or your position here. Starting from tomorrow, I will be Mr Tiverton, your colleague, and you will be Miss Littleworth, the esteemed Headmistress's substitute."

It would be a professional relationship of mutual esteem, respect—and distance.

It was a most sensible decision.

Frances nodded. "Thank you."

They stepped into the vestibule together. He gave a curt bow and left.

Frances stood alone in the dark hallway, allowing herself to recall what he'd whispered into her ear, one last time, before she'd banish the words, forever.

CHAPTER 10

*P*ercy paced his room restlessly and replayed the events of the previous evening in his mind.

It had been just a mistletoe kiss, by Jove! It was not only a practice that was commonly accepted but also expected. Tradition and all that. It would've reflected badly on a fellow to ignore that, especially if he stood right underneath a bough with a dashingly kissable girl.

However, he had to be honest with himself. The kiss wasn't the problem. The problem was what he'd blurted out afterwards.

What the deuce had got into him that he'd blurted *that* out? What had taken hold of him to say such an utterly hare-brained thing? He couldn't shake the feeling that she'd almost slapped him. No wonder she'd paled and literally run away from him.

If he could unsay those words, he would. Never mind that he felt there was some truth to them. Never mind that in the spur of the moment, he'd meant them with the entire fibre of his soul. Never mind that he'd never said those words to anyone before.

Still, he should not have said them. He tore at his hair. Dash it all.

Frances Littleworth. She was kind, caring and courageous, interesting to talk to, had a wonderful sense of humour, and her voice was divine. Those moments in the drawing room when she played and sang, and he was the only one in the room, were precious to him. Her voice inspired him, and he'd never painted as much, nor as well, as when he listened to her sing. She was his muse. What was more, he'd never felt so at home with anyone before.

And now, he'd never felt so awkward.

Now what?

He couldn't bear being in the same room with her. Not if his presence embarrassed her. The thought that she did not reciprocate his feelings pained him.

Neither could he bear being holed up in his room, where he was doomed to inevitable brooding. What to do?

He tore the door open and stepped out into the hallway. His eyes drifted over the wall over the staircase. It looked as if someone had recently picked off the old brown wallpaper that he'd seen in other parts of the house, whitewashed the walls, but had not got around to putting up new wallpaper. He remembered that fixing this wall would have been his assignment if he'd lost the cribbage wager.

FRANCES HAD HOLED HERSELF UP IN THE OFFICE AND HAD not emerged for either dinner or tea. She hadn't seen

Percy the entire day. She was not avoiding him, she told herself. She was just so very busy.

The memory of his slow, gentle kiss sang through her veins. A kiss as tender and light as a butterfly's wing.

She slammed down the box with chalk on the desk so hard that a puff of chalk dust rose. She coughed and slapped the chalk dust off her fingers.

It was just a mistletoe kiss.

It was meaningless. Like that first kiss had been, the one he'd won at cribbage. Also meaningless.

And this feverish feeling that grabbed her was maybe a sign that she was coming down with the flu. She placed the back of her hand against her forehead.

But then he'd said those words.

It had sent a vibe of shock through her entire being, because she had expected anything but that. The hammering of her heart, the jolt in her stomach, the shivery, weak feeling in her legs were surely all merely because it had been so unexpected.

She collapsed with a sigh in her armchair.

She was most definitely coming down with the flu.

Or else, falling in love.

She clawed her fingernails into the armrest.

No, no, no, no, and no!

This could not, would not, was not to be. She simply could not afford falling in love. It would be most inconvenient! She was well on her way to becoming Miss Hilversham's trusted and respected successor. She herself had hinted at this on more than one occasion, as Miss Hilversham was travelling more and more, looking for more challenges, setting up schools elsewhere. Who would take over seminary in Bath when she moved on for good? Why, she, Frances, of course. There was nothing Frances would love more. Her future would be made. It would be the pinnacle of all her dreams and desires.

She would not ruin it all by falling in love.

Especially with a man who was kind and sensitive and caring, one who listened with true interest to what she had to say, was charming and tolerably handsome, in fact, disturbingly so, since she could barely tear her eyes away from him lately.

She stopped in confusion and felt like slapping herself. She didn't even know him. Who was he, really? Where did he come from? Why was he here? He had secrets, she was sure.

She stepped into the hallway, turned towards the stairs, and grabbed the rail to make her way up. She paused half-way.

There he was, crouching on the stairs, a lamp beside him, his tousled head almost touching the ground. He was in shirts, his sleeves pushed up, and he held something in his left hand. Her heart jumped. He looked unbelievably handsome in his rumpled shirt and uncombed hair.

Then she gasped. Then she bent her head sideways and squinted. "Ooh," she sighed.

He saw her from his sideways position, scrambled up, and shot a crooked smile at her. "Good evening, Frances. I mean, Miss Littleworth."

She was incapable of replying.

"I thought I'd find myself some work to do." He gestured up the wall. "I found paint in one classroom. What do you think?" He looked at her eagerly.

He'd painted a mural in the style of Michelangelo.

From the boldly sketched outline, she could identify the heroes of Antiquity.

Frances pointed at a figure on a ship. "That is Odysseus." Her finger wandered on. "Achilles?"

Percy nodded, pleased. "The battle with Hector. And look. Here is the beautiful Helena."

Did Frances imagine it, or were Helena's features similar to hers?

"I also wanted to include the gods." Above a cloud-like image were Zeus, Hera, Ares, and Athena.

Frances sat down on the stair and leaned back against the railing, watching with an open mouth. It was like a picture book on the wall.

"This is like a history lesson on Greek mythology."

"I am glad you think so." He rubbed his neck. "This is the first time I am doing something like this, for the public. The idea is not for me to finish it, but to let our pupils complete the task."

"They will absolutely love it. And Miss Hilversham…" Sweet heavens. Miss Hilversham! What would she think?

"The strict headmistress." He tilted his head sideways in the manner that had begun to tug at her heart. "She won't object, will she?"

"I don't know. That is, I don't think so. It will be rather surprising to her to have her entire hallway transformed to this—" she waved her hand at the mural, "but I daresay in the end she will marvel at it like the rest of us."

"I think the good lady appreciates art and values the classics. I have been to the Lapidarium. It is brilliant."

The Lapidarium was one of the latest projects in which Miss Hilversham exhibited the Roman statues and artefacts that were found on the premises.

"Yes, interestingly enough, there must have been an ancient Roman villa here once, with statues and other artefacts. Miss Hilversham had them excavated and collected them all in that part of the garden. It is almost like an outdoor museum, is it not?"

"It is delightful. The heads of the statues are most interesting. They can serve as objects to be sketched. I will plan on taking the class to the Lapidarium to study Roman art. They will see first-hand what it was all about, touch the statues and vases, and then attempt to recreate them themselves. This is just a sample of what they will be able to do in the end."

"You have great faith in the talents of your fellow humans." She herself could sketch with the skill required of a female of her status, but she would never presume to call herself talented.

"My belief is that anyone can paint with excellent instruction. It is all a matter of training the eye to see."

He held out his hand and pulled her up. He had streaks of paint on his hand, and a blue streak right across his forehead.

"So you said." She could not tear her eyes away from him.

PERCY WORKED FURIOUSLY AT THE MURAL BUT LEFT IT ONLY half-painted. He washed his paint-streaked face and hands in the bowl in his room, satisfied. It had turned out rather better than what he'd first imagined. It was a glorious, tremendous painting from floor to ceiling, in the brightest colours, vibrant, alive with movement and story.

The maid, Martha, had stood in front of it with a

gaping mouth, and let the dustbin clatter to the floor. But Frances's reaction had pleased him more. It was what she'd not said that had pleased him. How her eyes had widened in childlike astonishment. How her soft lips had dropped open in a gentle O. How she couldn't stop looking at it, understanding the symbolism he'd worked into it. He'd studied her face as she'd studied his art, and he'd felt such deep emotion well up within himself that he'd almost shuddered.

He'd clasped his paintbrush so tightly he'd nearly broken it in half.

This Miss Littleworth, did she know what contradictory signals she was sending? First such care, when he was ill, almost motherly. Then the cool, businesslike manner of a manager, a headmistress. Then the childlike joy on her face when he'd prepared the Christmas dinner. The tears of gratitude in her eyes had almost unmanned him, and he'd almost cried along with her. The desire in her eyes when he'd kissed her. The cold, hard rejection when he'd forgotten himself and uttered the forbidden words. Then again, the look of open admiration on her face when she studied the mural.

It bothered him. Who, exactly, did she admire? Him, or his talent?

He fervently hoped it was him.

CHAPTER 11

The smell of burned greens lingered in the air. Anna and Martha had taken the Christmas greenery down and burned them in the fireplace on the day after Twelfth night. Gone was the mistletoe, gone was the holly. All that remained was ash.

Suddenly, the house was filled with the sound of trunks and crates scraping on the wooden floorboards, footsteps running up and down the stairs, excited chatter and laughter, and some quiet and not so quiet tears. The students had arrived.

Frances stood by the door and welcomed each student, greeted parents and guardians, and relished the expressions on their faces when they beheld the new mural on the wall.

The teachers Miss Robinson and Miss Brown had returned as well. Miss Ellen Robinson stood in the hallway, bringing in a flurry of snow, and widened her arms when she saw Frances.

"I must say, it is always a pleasure to return." She

smacked a kiss on each of Frances's cheeks. "As much as I love my family, my true home is here. In this school. With you all."

Only Miss Hilversham was still absent. She hadn't written for a while. Frances worried in earnest.

"What can be the matter?" She drew her eyebrows together. "The roads must still be blocked. I hope she hasn't fallen ill."

Frances had faithfully written her missives every second day, reporting on every single event at the school. Who fell sick, who was well again. She'd written that she'd hired Percy. Only about that mural in the wall she couldn't bring herself to write just yet. Miss Hilversham would have to see for herself. It was impossible to put into words.

PERCY—MR TIVERTON, SHE CORRECTED HERSELF IN HER mind, for they were to be on formal terms from now on— so, Mr Tiverton stood in his classroom for the first time, pale and excited. Earlier, he said his knees were knocking together from sheer terror, and she'd offered him some laudanum, which he'd waved away with disgust. "I shall fall asleep in my very first class, Miss Littleworth."

His behaviour towards her was correct, down to the very tip of his toes. Courteous, yet pleasantly cheerful, he treated Frances with the respect of a superior.

Frances sighed.

Then she pulled her shoulders back. It was the first day of school. And there was so much to do. She had more important things to think about than mistletoe kisses and promises.

In the afternoon, she quietly walked into Percy's classroom, sat in a chair beside the door, and listened.

The class was unusually quiet. Fifteen pairs of eyes were glued on him, as he told them in glowing terms about the Art of Raphael. He had books spread all over the desk, picked them up, and passed them about. He had visited the churches in Italy and seen many of the paintings first-hand.

"The Madonna del Prato, also known as the Madonna on the Meadow, is an oil painting which Rafael painted in Florence. It depicts the Virgin Mary with the Infant Jesus and John the Baptist. Rafael first sketched it in red chalk. We too, will first draw our preparatory sketches in chalk before we continue on to oils."

"But, sir, what are we to paint?" a girl with two black braids asked.

"Wherever inspiration takes you."

Fifteen pairs of open mouths gaped at him. "You mean, sir, that we can paint whatever we want to?"

"For the moment, the what is not as important as the how. We will practise the technique first, then you will each choose an overarching topic and attempt to express that in a drawing."

"But sir, what topic?"

"Felicitas Bentley, is it not? Kindly raise your hand before speaking. I suggest an allegorical topic, such as hope, faith, joy, or love. But you may also choose something else altogether."

Did Frances imagine it, or did he briefly lift his eyes to meet hers when he mentioned love? She must have imagined it, for he talked on.

"Sir? What about the mural outside? It is unfinished."

"You will be allowed to work on that project only after you have completed this first assignment."

Oh, he was good. Not only was he an excellent artist, but he would also make his way as a teacher as well. He had a quiet authority about him that made people listen to him when he spoke. He never needed to raise his voice. Frances decided that he'd passed his trial class with flying colours. She was glad, so glad. She was certain Miss Hilversham would approve of him, too.

PERCY LAY ON HIS BED, WITH HIS SHOES ON, AND STARED AT the ceiling. What a day it had been! He felt simultaneously exhilarated and drained. He had taught a class! He had really, and actually, instructed fifteen eager young people in the arts.

And he had survived. In fact, he'd not only survived, he'd been good at it! He drew his hands over his eyes. Who would have thought? He not only enjoyed teaching, but his pupils seemed to have actually enjoyed his lesson. They'd paid attention, they'd done what he told them to do. It was incredible! There was only one student who'd been sassy, that Felicitas Bentley, who'd initially resisted following his instructions and making a draft with the red chalk. She'd insisted on jumping over the draft and going directly to the oils. With the consequence that she'd botched up her painting hopelessly and had to start from scratch with a chalk draft by the time the others were ready to move on to oils.

Show me, then, that you are capable of fending for yourself! His father had snarled at him.

Percy clenched his hands into fists. "I am doing it," he

muttered. "I am doing it right now. I am proving to myself, to you, father, and to the entire world, that Percy Tiverton is capable of not only fending for himself, but living off his art. And not only that. He is teaching it to others!"

He felt such fierce pride rush through him; it made him almost giddy.

CHAPTER 12

*A*s the days passed, they settled into a comfortable routine. She loved watching him teach.

She also loved it when, after school hours, he joined her in the sitting room, listening to her whenever she played and sang. Sometimes for hours.

When she looked up, she saw his blond tousled head bent over a sketchbook.

When she asked him what he was drawing, he merely shook his head.

One particularly beautiful winter afternoon, Miss Brown asked for permission to take the children on an excursion to town. Miss Robinson would accompany them. So it came that Percy and Frances had an unexpected day off.

Since it was a cheerful January day, they took a turn in the garden conversing. Percy was an interesting conversationalist and easy to talk to. Whenever she said something, Percy bent down to her, his head slightly tilted, his hazel eyes thoughtful as he listened. Whatever doubts she may once have had regarding his education were long gone. She chuckled when she recalled the interview in which he'd come across as somewhat of a numbskull, no doubt just to tease her. Reality was, he was well read in the classics and exceptionally knowledgeable in art history. He talked with passion about the arts. When he described to her how the library of Alexandria must have looked like, she could almost see it in front of her.

"Mr Tiverton."

"Miss Littleworth." The teasing twinkle was back in his eyes, and Frances's heart soared.

"Are you happy teaching here?"

"I am enjoying every minute with my pupils. I did not know that teaching requires so many activities not related to teaching. It's dawned on me it isn't just about pressing information into those young minds, but also about shaping them into reasonable human beings with moral fortitude and integrity, responsible citizens who will leave a positive imprint on society and contribute towards making our world a better place one day. Once the gravity of this responsibility sank in, I grew rather terrified, I must admit."

"But this is what I love about this job. Helping shape young minds, their characters, and personalities. Helping unlock their potential so they can make their mark upon this world. Can there be a better vocation?"

"There isn't. I believe teachers to be the unsung heroes and heroines of this world."

"Which you are now one as well. For from what I have seen, you are truly excelling in this profession. I can't recall ever having a more popular instructor at this school."

He looked at her warmly. "That is because I have wonderful role models to follow. You are my inspiration, my muse."

Frances flushed. "Nonsense. It is all you and your own talent."

"You are an excellent teacher yourself, Miss Littleworth. You teach with heart and soul."

They'd wandered to the back of the garden, where the hedge separated the school grounds from the neighbour's land.

"Did you know that there is a wishing well in the neighbour's garden? They say it is a Celtic wishing well." Frances told him the story of four former pupils, and that their fates resulted from them having thrown coins down the well.

"I am not entirely sure I believe it myself, but it seems to be an odd coincidence that three of our students here ended up marrying dukes. The fourth one, to my knowledge, turned down a duke."

Percy laughed. "I would like to see this magical well. Do you think it is possible? That wishes come true by throwing coins into water?"

"I am not certain. Wouldn't it be wonderful if it were? Come, it is this way." She led him through the trees. "The house has been empty for years. No one wants to move in, maybe because they say it is haunted. I believe Miss Hilversham has, for a while, thought about buying it to expand the school grounds. I don't know what became of those plans. If we go here," Frances showed him the hedge, "And push this hedge aside, like this," she bent the branches aside, "it ought to be possible for us to squeeze through." She pressed herself through the narrow opening. Percy followed.

The wishing well was a rectangular pool made of marble hidden in a cove of trees at the back of the garden.

Percy inspected it. "It reminds me of the Roman baths in town, except smaller. I daresay the function may have been similar."

"Yet it is deeper than a bath." Frances bent over the side and looked down. The water was several feet beneath, and frozen. "Oh! What a shame. We can't throw any coins; they would land on the ice." While pulling herself up, she brushed against a branch, and it showered down snow.

Frances brushed it off with a laugh.

Percy stared. "For one moment, you looked like a snow queen." His eyes were filled with a curious deep longing. "You have a snowflake on your eyelash." He lifted his hand and touched Frances's eyelash.

Frances held her breath. His finger trailed down her cheek, to her left nostril, down to the curve of her lip. He bent his head. She stared at his lips. The air between them sizzled. She knew what was coming. "We shouldn't. Not again." She moistened her lips.

"No, we definitely shouldn't". He was so close, she could count the hair on his eyelashes. "It is a terrible idea."

"Yes," her breath quickened. "Terrible."

"What would Miss Hilversham say." His lips came closer.

"I could lose my position." She stared at the curve of his upper lip.

"Tell me to stop."

A brief shiver rippled through her. How her entire

being yearned for it. Why deny that what you want deep down, her heart whispered. She was so tired of fighting herself, her emotions, him. So tired.

"Kiss me," she whispered.

He tilted her chin up gently, and his lips came down coaxingly to cover hers. It was a delicious sensation that made her entire body sing. Finally, a real kiss, not a peg as a prize, nor an obligatory kiss demanded by tradition while other people watched and jeered in the background, but a proper kiss, coming from the soul. She threw all her fears and hesitations into the wind as she kissed him back with reckless abandon.

Nothing had ever felt so right.

He kissed the corner of her lips, the dimple in her chin, the pulsing hollow at the bottom of her exposed throat, for she'd dropped her shawl. "Frances, sweet Frances…" he murmured against her skin.

He clasped her to him tightly, his head leaning on hers, and she listened to the thumping of his heart, feeling something so powerful surge through her it brought tears to her eyes.

Would it be so terrible? To finally admit to it. To finally allow it.

Love.

She'd never felt more light, more joyful, more at peace.

Maybe it could work. Somehow.

A sparrow landed on a snowy branch above them and caused a bulk of snow to slide down over their heads.

They scattered apart with a laugh.

Frances lifted her hand and whisked the snow away from his hair. She took his hand and pressed a kiss on his palm. "Let us go inside and warm up with a cup of hot tea. Ellen will return soon with the students."

They returned to the hedge holding hands and stole bashful glances at each other when they approached the house.

Martha opened the door and ushered them into the vestibule. They stomped off the snow on the mat.

"There is a lady waiting for you in the reception room, Miss," Martha said as she took their coats. "She would not say who she is."

It happened frequently that former students visited unexpectedly, and to keep it a surprise, they did not want to be announced. Frances assumed it was such a student. "Show her into the other sitting room, please. It is warmer there since the fire is roaring in the fireplace, and I am fairly frozen to an icicle. Also, bring us some tea."

Percy stood in front of the fireplace and held out his fingers. "The cold makes my fingers stiff. I have to be careful. There is nothing worse for an artist than to have stiff fingers."

Frances was about to reply that he should've worn gloves, when a high-pitched female voice squealed, "Percy?"

He whirled around.

A lady in a white, fur-lined coat and a muff stood in the door, her pink lips forming a round O.

"Sophia!" Percy's face drained of blood.

"Oh, it is you! Percy!" The young woman tripped forward with a sob and threw herself around his neck. "I knew you would be somewhere, though I feared you dead, especially when the bow street runners could not come up with anything substantial." She blew her nose. "I am so glad I finally found you! It was Adkins who told everyone you were at this school in Bath. Everyone thought he was joking, but I did not."

Percy closed his eyes. "Adkins. Of course."

"How can you just disappear like that, terrible man! Though I am so glad you are not dead!" The woman embraced him anew.

Frances still held her scarf in her hand and stared at the embracing couple in front of her, feeling decidedly superfluous. Was the woman a relative? A cousin?

She cleared her throat gently.

Percy disentangled himself from her and avoided her eyes. "Sophia––Frances––I mean, Miss Littleworth." He stammered, looking from one to another. "This is Miss Frances Littleworth."

It looked like it took him every ounce of his willpower to pull himself together and face Frances. "May I present Miss Sophia Fielding." He closed his eyes for a moment. Then he took a big breath before adding quietly, "my fiancée."

CHAPTER 13

*H*er entire world tilted.

It seemed like time had suspended itself as the words slowly sank in, like barbs, into her very being, her very soul.

She was his fiancée, not his sister, as Frances had first assumed. He'd dropped that piece of information as if it were the most natural thing in the world, not knowing he'd just punched her in the gut and tore out her heart.

Frances gasped for breath.

Percy was engaged to be married. To someone else. To a gorgeous lady who was beautiful and, judging from her dress, evidently very rich, a lady of the highest rank. She was everything Frances was not.

Sophia did not even glance at Frances. She clutched Percy's hands and looked up into his face, tears still streaming down her cheeks.

"You shouldn't have come here, Sophia. All alone, in this weather." His voice sounded harsh in the room's silence.

"Percy." Sophia shook his arm like a little child, demanding attention.

"The carriage could've overturned, or you could've ended up snowed in somewhere, in some seedy inn." He never looked at Frances. Not even once. "Or something worse."

"Percy." Sophia took a big breath. "I had to come. I did not want the news to reach you first. It is your father, you see."

He looked down at her, his forehead knit into a steep frown. "Father?"

"I am so sorry, Percy." She looked at him with sorrow. "He is dead."

THERE WAS NO SOUND IN THE ROOM OTHER THAN THE crackle of the fire. Percy's face had been white before, but now he looked positively gutted.

"Father is dead?"

"They say his heart failed. I am so sorry, Percy." Sophia wept quietly into her handkerchief.

Normally, Frances would've walked over and consoled him. But that was no longer her right. It would never be her right.

She forced herself out of her stupor, pulled herself up, and wrapped her arms about her middle for support. "My condolences, Mr Tiverton." Her voice sounded wooden.

Sophia lowered her handkerchief. "The Viscount of Ingleby is now the Earl of Halsford," she informed Frances.

Frances's breath shook as she exhaled. "I see. I will give you some privacy and leave you with your f-f-fiancée."

Percy turned and finally looked at her, but it did not appear he'd heard what she just said.

She left the room, closed the door behind her quietly and returned to her room. There, she sat down on her bed.

Breathe, Frances. Breathe.

There were no tears. Only an icy, painful clump of dread and pain in the pit of her stomach that churned, that grew, that reached for her heart.

After a while of sitting dry-eyed, but stunned, on her bed, she got up. She was a headmistress here. She had responsibilities. Squaring her shoulders, she left the room to go to the office.

After several hours of work, someone tapped on the door.

She did not lift her head when the door opened, closed, and when footsteps approached and stopped in front of her desk.

After a while, she looked up.

His eyes were full of such stark sorrow that she nearly lost her calm. With steely resolve, she set aside her quill. "Please. Have a seat."

The chair scraped on the floor as he pulled it aside.

"Frances—"

"So the Earl of Halsford was your father. I am sorry for your loss, my lord. May I express my condolences on behalf of the entire school and its staff."

"Please. Call me Percy." His voice was pleading.

She brushed it aside. She pulled out the top drawer with a jerky motion and withdrew an envelope and handed it to him.

He stared at it. "What is this?"

"The salary that is due to you. Note it isn't the full salary a senior teacher receives, as we agreed you teach here on a trial basis only until Miss Hilversham confirms your position. However, this point now is, I assume, moot."

He did not pick up the envelope.

She placed it on the table. "Well? This is what you have wanted all the time. Take your earnings, my lord."

"Frances. I am so very sorry."

"You are sorry." Frances's breath quickened as anger flushed through her. "Whatever for, I wonder? For all the lies you told? That you were not an artist, but a nobleman? That you led us all to believe you were sincere about following the profession as a drawing master? That you've been engaged to be married to someone else this entire time?" Her voice broke. "Pray, what else haven't you told me that I should know?"

He tried to grab her hand on the table, but she pulled it away. "I have no excuses. There are no words. I have deceived you grossly. For this, I apologise sincerely. There is nothing I can say that will change the facts of my life, no matter how hard I try to ignore and outrun them."

"It isn't that you tried to forget your identity by pretending to be someone else that I have issues with. The rich, pampered viscount finds himself bored in the clubs of London and runs away to play at being a drawing master." She tapped her finger on the table. "On some level, this is almost understandable. Amusing, even."

He winced.

"But no, it is not this that I object to. It is that you were engaged to be married to someone else. This entire time. You led me to believe that you were not. That your heart was free." She whispered the last words. "I find this unforgivable."

"It sounds absolutely terrible the way you put it, but I will not dispute it." He looked at her unhappily. "I should have told you earlier. I merely resulted in making a mess of it all in a dishonourable manner."

"You are correct." Frances's voice shook. "An honourable man does not behave in this way. Being engaged to one woman and kissing another."

He flushed.

"Was it all a grand joke to you, then?"

"No, Frances, never a joke. Please—"

"My name is Miss Littleworth."

"Miss Littleworth, dash it. I have misled you grossly. I apologise. But I have always been truthful about my feelings. I have my reasons, if you would let me explain—"

"I don't want to hear it," she cut him off. He was engaged to be married to someone else. What was there to explain? So, it had all been meaningless flirtation. The magic they shared, nothing but an illusion. She'd been a fool to have believed in the truth of it for even a second.

"I think you have explained quite enough," she repeated.

Percy slumped in his chair. "I need to return to London. I need to sort this out. Sophia… she is waiting. I have family obligations, Frances. Miss Littleworth. Obligations and responsibilities that they have given me since birth and that I never wanted. I can't run away from them, even though I tried." He rumpled his hair. "By Jupiter, how I tried."

"I understand perfectly."

He lowered his hands and looked at her with sadness. "I wish we could part on better terms."

Frances did not know where she found the strength to get up, gripping the edge of the desk for support. "I bid you Godspeed, Mr Tiverton. It has been a pleasure having you here, as short as it was. You were a be-beloved teacher here. Pray do not return."

She turned around and stared out of the window.

"Frances—" He stood up, sighed. Lifted his hand. Dropped it again. "I have misled you in many things. But not in one. Never in that. You *must* believe me."

She did not turn around.

The soft click of the door let her know that he'd left.

She held her breath for several minutes longer before she buried her head in her arms and sobbed her heart out.

He had not taken the envelope.

CHAPTER 14

When Miss Hilversham returned from the North two weeks later, she encountered a well-run school, happy, well-fed, studious pupils, and a head teacher who looked gaunt and had deep, dark rings under her eyes.

There was also the outline of an outrageous mural on the wall up the stairs that hadn't been there before.

"Goodness gracious," Miss Hilversham exclaimed, and she never exclaimed anything. "This looks like it's a copy of the Sistine Chapel, except," she pushed up her spectacles and bent forward to inspect Zeus, "it seems to be entirely mythological. Thankfully, these characters are all properly clad and not parading about in nudity like they are wont to do." She sniffed. "Do you care to explain, Frances?"

Frances tugged at her skirt with skittish fingers and avoided her eyes. "It was Mr Tiverton, you see."

"Ah. The paragon of a male teacher. Your letters were full of our newest colleague. An artist, I seem to recall.

No doubt he must have painted this. How very well done. He is extraordinarily talented. Where is he?" She looked up and saw Ellen shrug, and Frances stare at the carpet on the stairs as if it were the most interesting thing ever.

"It is a long story," she eventually said.

"I see. Shall we proceed to my office, where you will tell me all about it?"

Martha served tea, and after she'd left, Frances told her the entire story, from the moment Percy had arrived to the moment he'd suddenly left. She skipped the part with the ball and the mistletoe promise. Her heart ached every time she thought of it.

Miss Hilversham stirred thoughtfully in her cup. Her blonde hair was so light it was almost silvery, and the spectacles on her narrow nose made her look older than she was. In reality, she was merely a few years older than Frances, in her early thirties.

"An earl, you said?" She wrinkled her forehead in distaste. "This Mr Tiverton has misled you—misled us—grossly. He is exactly the kind of person I should have warned you against. When one posts advertisements in the newspaper, one attracts all sorts of people. Suddenly, anyone wants to try their hand at teaching, especially at a seminary as exclusive as ours. He was clearly never committed to this position. We cannot afford to waste our time and energy on people like that."

"But Mr Tiverton was truly an excellent teacher. He is not only a talented artist but also gifted with the ability to teach his craft to others. He worked as hard as any of us, and he made a difference in the few weeks he was here. The girls miss him and are determined to finish the projects he's assigned them." Frances couldn't help but defend him.

Miss Hilversham pursed her lips. "Be that as may. We are left to replace him, in addition to finding a replacement for Miss Keating. Have there been any applicants?"

Frances shook her head. "None that are useful."

Miss Hilversham frowned. "We need to find new staff soon. I see you are on the verge of collapsing. You are overworked, and I don't want you falling ill. How many hours have you slept last night?"

Frances chewed on her lips thoughtfully before replying, "I think four."

It was a lie. Frances had lost the ability to sleep. For when she did, her dreams were feverish and filled with Percy's laughing face. So, she remained awake, thrashing about, replaying each memory, each word. In the mornings, her pillow was damp with tears. But she'd never tell that to anyone, of course.

"Get some rest at once. I cannot have my best teacher fall out as well. Ellen should take over your classes in the afternoon."

Frances did as she was told; however, she lay awake in bed. When Martha came to deliver her mail, she seized it gladly, only to scold herself for raising her hope every time.

He would never write. Of course, he shouldn't. It was for the best.

And yet, this tiny spark of hope, that there would be a missive for her lying on the silver tablet, written in his handwriting….

Instead, there was a letter from London, in an unfamiliar handwriting.

Dearest great-niece,
You cannot imagine my delight at having received your letter.
Your mother, God bless her soul, was not only my favourite
niece, but also a friend. I will never understand certain
members of this family who have deemed it necessary to cut off
communication merely because she married beneath her station.
For one does not choose who one falls in love with.

Frances closed her eyes painfully.

I am therefore delighted that you have written, and I am
delighted to learn that your brother Nathaniel is in London. Of
course, a young man like him will get himself into all sorts of
trouble without the right guidance. Fear not. I will take him
under my wings. I also expect you to come for a visit. This
meeting is overdue.
Affectionately yours,
Polly

Frances lowered the letter. It had been Percy who'd encouraged her to write to great-aunt Apollonia. So much had happened in the meantime that she'd all but forgotten about it. So, now her great-aunt wanted her to go to London?

She picked up a second letter, which was from Nat.

Sister dear,
I have wonderful news. Our great-aunt Apollonia has been in
contact with me. You may recall that she is mother's aunt. Even
though our relationship to mother's family has been as good as
nonexistent, they have been surprisingly gracious about
receiving me. Great-aunt Apollonia especially wants to renew

contact with us and insists we visit. She very much wants to get
to know you.
Do say you'll come? I am missing you greatly.
With affection, your brother
Nat

Frances's mind whirled. Her mother had mentioned Apollonia being the eccentric one of the family. Apparently, she'd been the only one who stood up to the family saying the ostracism of their mother was unwarranted simply because she'd married a commoner.

Mother, however, had been very cross and cut off everyone, including great-aunt Apollonia.

Thus, it came that Frances and Nat grew up without ever having met their relatives.

Frances tapped the quill against her lips. Visiting her great-aunt in London. Was that a good idea? Her first impulse was to decline. It was out of the question, for she was much needed here. If she went, there would only be two teachers left to teach. That would never work.

To her big surprise, Miss Hilversham listened quietly to Frances when she told her about the letter.

"You must go, Frances. Not only because you need to make peace with that part of the family, but also because you badly need to get away from here."

Frances sat up with a jolt. "Pardon me?"

"Yes. You heard right. You need to leave the school for a while. It will do you good. Trust me, I am speaking from experience." She smiled wryly.

"But I love this school! I love being here. I love teaching!"

"Yes, you do. You love it with every fibre of your being,

so much so that you are doing nothing else, living, breathing for this school. In other words, you are wasting away." She threw Frances a sharp look. "Nothing, and no one, is worth wasting away for. Not this school, not our students, wonderful as they are. Least of all a man."

Frances's mouth dropped open.

"I am not blind, child." Miss Hilversham placed a cool hand over Frances's, which twitched underneath. "I know you are suffering from a broken heart. You need to go away and heal it. And when you have done so, you may come back and return, with renewed vigour, to your teaching."

"But you need me here. There isn't enough staff. How will you cope?"

"I will cope very well without you, Frances, mind you. We have," she tapped on a pile of papers, "the last time I counted, thirty-four applications to the last advertisement I placed in *The Times*. I will hire a substitute for you while you are in London. You are to take off not only Easter but also the summer. I don't want to see you back until next term."

Frances's eyes filled with tears. "You are sending me away. You want to replace me."

"Nonsense. You are to leave to regenerate your spirit. You're turning into a wraith in front of my very eyes, and I can't have that." She pulled out a handkerchief and handed it to Frances, who suddenly found she could no longer keep the tears from flowing. She pressed her eyes.

"Sometimes crying is the best thing we can do, indeed. You will feel so much better afterwards. Then you will pack your suitcase and visit your great-aunt. I expect a weekly report." She'd said that with a slightly humorous undertone.

Frances blew her nose. "I will. Maybe you are right. I haven't seen Nat in ages and miss him terribly. And I suppose it is time for us to get to know my mother's family. Family is family, after all. And they say London is full of libraries and museums. I will return with wonderful teaching material."

"Don't forget the most important thing, Frances: to enjoy yourself," Miss Hilversham said with a smile.

Frances doubted she would, but now a sense of excitement took hold of her. She had never been to London.

It would help distract her.

It would help her forget *him*.

CHAPTER 15

*G*reat-aunt Apollonia.

Oh my! She was as un-auntly as an aunt could possibly be. Lady Apollonia Watling dyed her hair a bright copper and dressed youthfully in the newest fashion, with heavy flounces and flares, bright floral patterns and puffed-up sleeves. Her hats were the size of carriage wheels and heavily draped with ribbons, feathers and lace. She carried gloves, a reticule and a moss-green umbrella with her wherever she went.

"One never knows when it rains," she declared.

When Frances stepped off the carriage in front of her home in Berkeley Square, her great-aunt emerged from the front door with the umbrella and began talking to her as if they'd stopped mid-conversation.

"You cannot, for the life of me, tell me it won't rain." Her eyes fixated on the sky as she held her hand out.

Frances blinked. "I can't do what?"

"What did I say? I felt a drop. Come in, child, you will get soaked in a minute." She ushered Frances up the stairs to the front door, where she paused. "There. Goodness, you look like your blessed mother. May she rest in peace. The same complexion. The same nose. No. The nose must be from your father. It is the eyes. Bless you if that isn't Charity looking right at me. Where is my handkerchief? I have something in my eye. It is getting all teary. But look at you! Is this how you dress in Bath? My dear girl! I see we shall have to go shopping."

Frances embraced her great-aunt. She did not know whether to laugh or cry. The unexpected reference to her mother made her miss her mother fiercely.

"Did you have a pleasant trip? Never mind answering, I see you are tired and wan. The trip must have been horrid. Terrible roads, I say. All these turnpikes! Come inside and have some tea. There, what did I say? It's veritably pouring." She opened her umbrella for the two last steps into the house. The fat raindrop that landed on her nose implied that her great-aunt was correct about the weather.

Apollonia had a parrot in the drawing room, a Siamese cat and a pug dog, who sat on a silken cushion on the sofa and glared at her malevolently.

"Never mind Prinny. Just don't sit beside him, he will bite," she declared and kissed the dog.

"Prinny? Did you say you named him Prinny?"

"Prinny, may he live and thrive, because he's at least as fat as the man. Now even more so that he's king. We have a full programme," she said in the same breath.

"Programme? Programme for what?"

"Balls, parties, picnics, for starters." Apollonia gestured for her to sit.

Frances stared at her, aghast. "But I am here to visit

you and Nat, not go to any balls. I am not prepared at all to go dancing."

"Nonsense, of course you have to go to balls. Why would you want to visit an old woman like me? To sit around and do embroidery? No, no. You have to go to balls and enjoy the season as much as you can."

"The season? Great-aunt Apollonia—"

"Do leave off this great-aunt business, I beg you. It makes me feel positively ancient. What do they call those wrinkly things they found in Egypt?"

Frances blinked. "Wrinkly things? Egypt? Oh. You mean, mummies?"

"Yes, horrid things. All shrivelled up. Why am I talking about mummies? Oh, I recall. I meant to say I am not a mummy. Not yet at least, and I shan't ever be one, not if I can't help it. Make sure to always slather Olympian Dew on your skin. It will keep you from shrivelling up yourself. So do me a favour, leave off the 'great-aunt' and for heaven's sake, never call me Apollonia. Just call me Polly."

"Polly."

"There. That wasn't so difficult, was it?"

For the first time in weeks, Frances smiled. "Polly. I am so glad to know you. Finally."

"You are Charity's child. We shall get along famously."

"Is Nat coming soon?"

"The sweet boy is to come down from Cambridge tomorrow. Or so he says. We shall not be at home, however."

"We shan't?" It was exhausting following Polly's train of thought.

"No. We have a picnic at—oh dear. I forget the name.

Hindley!" She snapped her fingers and her butler appeared.

"Yes, my lady."

"Where do we have this picnic tomorrow? At the Whistleboroughs or at Lady Jersey's? Or was it the other one? What's the name? Ah. I know. Melbourne?"

Frances paled. Even she recognised the names of the most exclusive families in London.

"Great-aunt—I mean, Polly," she whispered, "what on earth have you been planning?"

"It is a dinner invitation from Lady Westington's, where Lady Lieven is to attend as well," the butler replied.

"Ah yes. I remember. It is going to be a dreadfully dull affair. That dinner, all they ever do is talk politics, but the whole point is that we wheedle Lady Lieven into obtaining us vouchers for Almack's. Equally dull affair, but I am afraid, necessary."

"Almack's!" Frances was speechless. What on earth was she to do there? Was Polly planning on marrying her off at that notorious marriage mart? She was far too old for that.

"Don't you worry, I have taken care of everything." Polly patted her cheek. "Go to your room and have some rest, then we will be off shopping." She picked up the pug from the cushion and whirled out of the room with the energy of a younger person.

"If you will follow me to your room," the housekeeper, who was waiting for her by the door, said.

"These will be interesting days," Frances muttered, forgetting that both housekeeper and butler were within hearing.

"Yes, Miss. If I may give some advice, it would be to

humour her ladyship and not to put up any resistance. It makes her even more stubborn."

"Thank you, Mrs—" Frances looked questioningly at the housekeeper.

"Mrs Roberts."

FRANCES AND POLLY TOOK A WALK IN THE PARK THE NEXT day. Armed with her umbrella in one hand, and Prinny's leash in the other, her great-aunt told her that Prinny needed to take a walk at least three times a day, and she did not trust anyone but herself to do it. Frances observed with amusement that Prinny did not look like he took very many walks, as he waddled along with his short legs and, after a while, plopped down and refused to move altogether. Polly picked him up and carried him for the rest of the walk.

Frances had written her letters to Miss Hilversham earlier, reporting as promised. She'd also met her brother Nat, whom she almost did not recognise. He was taller than she remembered. He held himself straight, and there was a self-confidence about him he'd lacked when he was younger. Cambridge, evidently, suited him. He was also dressed according to the newest fashion, in brown half-coat and pantaloons. He looked handsome and smart. So, this is where her hard-earned money went, she thought wryly. He'd hugged his sister affectionately.

"I will finish university by the end of summer, and I have a position as a junior partner in a law firm on hold," he told her. "They are quite interested in having me join their team."

"Oh, Nat, that is wonderful news indeed!" Frances clasped her hands.

"Polly somehow pulled some strings. Did you know that her husband, our uncle Richard, before he died, had considerable influence in the banking and law world? You no longer need to send me your money. I will not have it. Now is the time for me to take care of you, sister dear. I wouldn't be where I am without you. You made it all possible."

Frances shook her head. "No. I am well off, Nat. I don't need anyone to take care of me."

"Are you happy, Frances?" He gave her a searching look. "I know the times after mother and father passed were difficult for you when you laboured for the both of us."

Frances hesitated a moment before answering. "Of course, I am happy, silly. I love my work."

"So you say, but sometimes I wonder... whether you aren't using your work as an excuse to avoid..." his voice trailed off.

"Avoid what?"

"You'll be cross." A dimple appeared on his cheek when he smiled. "But very well, I'll say it. I am afraid that you are using your work as an excuse to avoid living. That's all."

Frances rubbed her eyebrow. "Of course that's silly. I'm here, after all, am I not? Polly has a long string of dinners, balls and banquets planned for us."

Nat nodded. "Yes, this is why I am so glad you came. You will enjoy yourself, you will see."

"That remains to be seen," Frances muttered.

Nat left for the club, cheerfully twirling his stick.

CHAPTER 16

*P*ercy Basil Tiverton, Earl of Halsford, drove his fiancée, Sophia Fielding, in a curricle through Hyde Park. To any outsider, he gave the impression of listening attentively to her chatter about the weather, the *ton,* and everything else under the sun. Sophia was an amiable girl of a good family; she not only had good breeding but also looked good, with her blonde corkscrew curls and light blue dress. Yes, Sophia surely was… good. He really couldn't think of another adjective that described her better. She was goodness in person, Percy thought. It was odd, because for when it came to Frances, he could think of a wide range of adjectives that described her. "Good" would've been too bland a word. She was so much more than that. He'd noticed everything about her, the precise shade of her eyes, how the light played on her hair, the curve of her lips. How she tilted her head sideways when she listened to him. Underneath her sweet exterior, Frances was all passion, excitement, eagerness about what she did, about her students, and life. And when she sang…

"Percy?"

"Hm?"

Sophia looked at him oddly.

He returned to her with a jolt. "I'm sorry, dear. Did you say something?" Dash it, but he sounded avuncular. He had to tune down that false heartiness in his tone. No wonder there was this peculiar expression on her face every time she looked at him lately.

"Three times already, Percy. Three times I asked you whether you look forward to the ball tomorrow evening."

"The ball. Is there a ball?" Upon seeing her face, he sat up. "Of course there is. Dash it if I haven't forgotten."

"I have been talking about nothing else for the past half hour!" Sophia pouted.

"So you have." He cleared his throat. This wasn't going well at all. He had to try harder. "So. The ball. We are going, aren't we? I mean, of course we are." He groaned inwardly. Why was conversing with Sophia so deucedly difficult?

Sophia stared at him. "I understand your father's passing quite distressed you. It was a shock to you. Do you feel it is too early for you to go to balls? You are still in mourning. Of course, it isn't expected of you to dance. But I would understand if you preferred not to go. Everyone would understand."

Here was his chance. To blazes with the dratted ball. He could call it off, blame it all on mourning his deceased father, and he could lock himself into his studio and paint until his brain steamed and his hand cramped. It had been the only thing that had seen him through the last few months that had kept him relatively sane. He'd locked himself in, and his butler and housekeeper had repeatedly attempted to lure him out by leaving trays of food in front of the door.

He hadn't eaten for days. Eventually, he'd collapsed and fallen into a deep sleep on the hard floorboards.

His butler had woken him up by shaking his shoulder. "My lord. Wake up. Your fiancée is here to see you."

Sophia. His fiancée.

Not Frances.

Never Frances.

He repressed the dull pain in his heart.

He'd scrambled up and tucked his shirt into his pantaloons when she breezed into the room, all pretty and cheerful and *good*.

"Oh, Percy," she'd whispered.

"Hello, Sophia." He cleared his throat and raked his hands through his dishevelled hair. He was unshaved, unwashed and likely looked a fright. "Do you want to go out on a ride?" He'd have to change first, for Sophia ought not to have a scarecrow sitting next to her in the curricle.

He'd never thought of her as his fiancée, even though his father had insisted on the engagement with Sophia, who was his best friend's daughter, years ago. The union of the two families being of utmost significance, and so forth. Percy had not minded. He'd known Sophia since she was in her lead-strings. They'd grown up with the expectation of getting engaged. So, when the time came, he went along with the engagement.

It was only when his father insisted he give up his art as if it were something shameful, and take up his seat in parliament, and get serious about becoming the future

Earl, that he thought about what that meant for the rest of his life.

He would marry Sophia, and he would be an earl, and he would step into his father's footsteps, like he did in his father's and so forth, for generations. He would never be what he dreamed most of being: an artist. He could never try what he'd been itching to try, whether he could earn his living with his art. It was preposterous for a man of his station to even think about, for aristocrats could never be men of trade. They did not earn their living through work. They did not even think of working. And in his case, it was not even a proper trade he held, but art. Something entirely useless. He'd felt the iron fetters clash down around him with a finality that caused him to break out in a cold sweat.

"I want to paint," he'd told his father. "I want to make my way through life with my art. Not the privilege of my title."

His father had smiled contemptuously. "Let me see if I understand you correctly. Rather than take your rightful place that you have been born into, you prefer to work like a commoner, dabble around with your drawings, sell a drawing or two on the streets. You will end up in the gutter, starving, living with the rats, and you shall be no better off."

This pricked Percy's pride. "I don't dabble. I can take on commissions. Get patrons. Get pupils. Teach."

His father had laughed. "Teach! Even worse. Who do you want to teach? And what patrons? Should the Duke of Ashmore hire you to paint his chapel? Like a common worker? Do you want to teach watercolours to his infant daughter? Eh? Be reasonable."

Percy clenched his hands. "I am reasonable. Common workers do not paint chapels. Highly talented artists do."

"Talent, pshaw. Workers. Artists. They're one and the same."

"With all due respect, sir, but they are not the same."

"Then prove it to me," his father flared up. "Prove me, then, that you can fend for yourself!"

How they had fought. Good heavens. His father had shouted at him with such fury that a spray of spittle had showered his face. "Go then! Get out of my sight. You can run all you want. When you are done running, you will realise that you cannot outrun your heritage, your identity, your very self. You have been and always will be the son of an earl. You are a lord of the land. It is a bloody privilege! You are not a—a—bloody artist starving in the gutter." He'd spat out the word. ´

His hand shook as he wiped his brow, remembering the angry words he'd hurled back at his father.

But he'd proven himself that he could do it. He'd found Miss Hilversham's advertisement in *The Times* and left for Bath without telling his father goodbye.

And now his father was dead.

His father would never know that he'd proven himself that he could do it.

But it had all been a dream. All that remained now was duty, responsibility, and a crushing sense of guilt. He had to maintain the earldom and take care of Sophia.

His father had been right. He could not run away from his heritage.

And he had to tear Frances out of his heart.

"Percy."

He looked up, startled.

"Yes, I am still here. Sitting beside you on the curricle." Sophia smiled wryly.

"I am sorry, Sophia." He shook his head with a sigh. "I am out of it. My mind is everywhere and nowhere."

"I have noticed." She played around with the sunshade. "May I ask you something?"

"Hm? I mean, yes, of course. Ask anything you want."

Sophia took a big breath. "Do you love her?"

Percy gripped the harness. "What?"

"The one you keep drawing over and over again. What was her name again? She was at that seminary in Bath. I saw her only briefly."

"I am not sure who you mean," he stammered.

"Oh, don't deny it, Percy. I am not blind. I have seen your drawings. All those pencil sketches. The floor in your drawing room is littered with crumpled paper balls, and they all depict her face. An ethereally beautiful face. Not in a physical sense, but you have somehow caught her inner beauty. She shines from within."

"Not quite. I can't seem to catch her essence, her soul. That glow. That softness. But also strength. It eludes me." His voice was full of despair. What if he failed to capture it before he forgot what she looked like? He did not want to talk about Frances to her. The Christmas magic they'd experienced. How for one moment he'd believed he could have it all. His life as an artist, a teacher... and Frances.

"You love her." Her voice was quiet, factual. "Oh, don't look so horrified. It is written all over you. And whatever it is you aren't saying, you are expressing on paper."

"Sophia." His voice was hoarse. "I don't know what to say."

"Then say nothing at all. But continuing on as we've

done up to now, pretending nothing is the matter, is not working, either. I deserve more, don't you think?"

His mouth moved, but no words came out.

"I also deserve love." Sophia set her chin up stubbornly. "I know that isn't something we commonly ask for nor expect in our circle as we enter marriage. Your father was practical when he insisted we get engaged. It would suit our families very well. But would it suit us? At first, I thought it could. We were always friends, weren't we? I thought maybe, one day, we could grow to love one other." She looked at him wistfully. "But it isn't to be, is it?"

Good heavens. What was she saying? "But Sophia. I am certain we can grow very fond of each other, eventually. I mean, we already are. Fond of each other, of course. Always have been. Aren't we? Dash it." He was evidently talking drivel.

Judging from the way Sophia looked at him, she seemed to think so, too. "Percy. Being fond of each other and being in love with each other isn't exactly the same."

No, it was not.

He pulled the curricle to a halt and stared blindly into the distance. "I am so sorry, Sophia. You are right. You deserve better. I wish things weren't as they are. I wish I didn't feel as I did. I wish, oh, I wish life weren't so complicated."

She set her hand on his. "I release you from our engagement, Percy."

"Sophia. No. Think of what will happen if you do this."

She shrugged. "What do you think will happen?"

"Your reputation. The talk." He shook his head. "I can't allow it."

"I don't fear it. I will tell everyone I changed my mind. That it was me who released you, not the other way around."

Percy looked at her, troubled.

"The gossip and rumours will blow over eventually. I'd rather take on several months of discomfort than an entire life of unhappiness. For I believe, as fond as we are of each other now, we will make each other very unhappy later."

He swallowed convulsively. Then he nodded curtly.

She held out her hand. "Let us shake hands and part as friends."

He lifted her hand, and, for the last time, planted a kiss on its back. "You have a noble soul, Sophia."

"Farewell, Percy." She sounded a little sad. "You deserve to be happy. But then, so do I."

PERCY USUALLY AVOIDED CLUBS, FOR THEY HELD NOTHING but gambling, drinking and coarse talking. But tonight, he decided he would go to his club and get roaring drunk.

But the moment he settled in the armchair in front of the fireplace, with a decanter of brandy in one hand and a glass in the other, he was accosted by a group of gentlemen.

"Halsford!" A hand slapped on his shoulder. "Well met. Where have you been these past few months? One hears all sorts of things." The young man who accosted him was Lord Ainsley, a dandy with whom he'd studied together at Cambridge. He was in the company of Lord Barington, also a Cambridge colleague, and a young gentleman whom he did not know.

"Barington. Ainsley." Percy gave them a slightly pained smile. He supposed it was too much to ask to be left alone.

"All alone here? We will join you, won't we?" They pulled up chairs and arranged themselves about him.

"How is your painting getting along? Halsford here is one of the most talented painters in the country," Ainsley said. "Scribbled his notebooks full instead of learning the law. Remember when the professor said if you can't focus on what he's saying that you should just leave? And you know what he did?" He looked around the group, laughing. "He said, 'well, then I'll leave', packed up his things and left! The professor was flabbergasted for an entire full five minutes." Ainsley slapped Percy on the shoulder.

"This sounds like Professor Wilkes," the young gentleman contributed. He seemed a dapper young man with easy-going manners. "I have him as well. A bit of a bore."

"It was Wilkes." Percy took a gulp from his brandy glass and looked at him, interested. "Are you from Cambridge, too? I don't think we've met before."

"My bad, Halsford. My bad," Ainsley said. "Let me make the introductions. This is Mr Nathaniel Littleworth. Littleworth, the Earl of Halsford."

The young man, with slightly flushed cheeks, jumped up and gave a small bow. "It is an honour, my lord."

Percy's knuckles whitened around his glass. "Littleworth."

"He's a bit of a greenhorn, aren't you, Little? Still acquiring some town bronze, he is. But he's a splendid chap and great fun to have about. Has good taste in tailors, too."

"You said your name is Littleworth?" Percy stared at him intently.

"Yes, my lord."

Percy lifted a finger and beckoned him to bend forward. "Do you have a sister?" he murmured, so the others, who were still joking about, did not hear.

Nat looked at him, surprised. "Indeed. Her name is Frances. Do you know her?"

CHAPTER 17

*S*he really did not want to go to that dinner. Aside from her great-aunt and Nat, she would not know a soul. It wasn't her circle. And what did she have to talk about, other than topics pertaining to school? She doubted anyone would be interested in talking about teaching methods or curriculums.

Frances pulled an apricot-coloured shawl over her shoulders. She wore an exquisite dress Polly had insisted on buying for her. It was silk and flowed about her limbs like water. It was tied under her breast with a sash in the back. The colour was a deep emerald green embroidered with leaves and paisleys.

Polly had taken one look at her, turned, and marched out of the room.

Well. She was no longer surprised by her great-aunt's eccentric behaviour, but sometimes it was difficult to understand her. Frances sat down on the sofa in the drawing room and waited for her.

Polly returned after several minutes, bearing in her hand a silver hair comb.

"Your outfit isn't complete without this." She handed her the comb.

Frances took it. "How pretty it is! It's almost like a snowflake."

"I daresay it is. I used to wear it frequently when I was a young girl. Then another young girl came and kept borrowing it from me. Your mother. Turn around." Frances did as she was bid. Polly gently placed the comb into the back of her head. "There. Perfection."

Frances felt a knot of tears in her throat. "Thank you, Polly. You've been more than kind to us. Oh dear. Now I am getting all weepy."

"Don't, for pity's sake. Don't. It will make your eyes red and puffy. That won't do. Now. Do you think it will rain tonight? For I had better bring my umbrella just in case. Ah. I hear Nat has arrived. Now we can leave together for that dinner. I expect it to be dreadfully dull."

Frances quickly dabbed at the corner of her eyes with a handkerchief and put up a smile as Nat entered the room.

"Polly! Frances. Are you all ready? Look who I have brought along."

There, behind Nat, tall and lanky as ever, was the Earl of Halsford.

Frances dropped her reticule.

Polly clapped her hands together. "Halsford! My, you have grown. The last time I saw you, you were in your lead-strings." She held out her hand, and Percy bowed over it.

"Lady Watling. It is a pleasure. I remember a picnic

where you brought along a parrot and a donkey, so I must have outgrown my lead-strings by then, as I remember riding the donkey."

"That must have been Napoleon and Josephine," Polly mused. "I remember. Such tragic deaths. Josephine flew away one day and got shot down by a hunter, and Napoleon died of heart failure. I daresay he was heart-broken at the loss. That was long before Prinny."

"Prinny being the dog over there, not the Prince Regent," Nat explained, pointing at the sofa, where Prinny rolled over with a snore.

Frances, after a moment of frozen shock, had picked up her reticule and felt the colour return to her cheeks. Her heart thumped wildly in her chest.

Nat chattered happily on. "I met Halsford in the club. We had the same professors at Cambridge. This is my sister. Turns out you two know each other?"

She found her hand taken in a tight grip. "Miss Littleworth."

She curtsied, murmured something in reply, and fixed her eyes doggedly on the golden button of his waistcoat.

Nat had recounted how, in the club, they discovered they had the same dinner invitation. "Then my lord offered to take us in his carriage so we could go together."

"It is very charming and thoughtful of his lordship," Polly's feathers on her head bobbed up and down as she nodded at him. "I daresay his carriage is more comfortable than ours. Well, what are we waiting for?"

Percy bowed in her direction. "It is a pleasure to be of service to you... and to Miss Littleworth."

· · ·

PERCY AND FRANCES SAT OPPOSITE EACH OTHER IN THE
carriage. Frances was careful to draw her knees aside lest
they touched his long ones.

His features were pale, his eyes dark and intense.

She felt his gaze on her the entire trip. Frances
strained her neck by pointedly looking outside the
window. Her mind reeled with confusion.

Why had he come? Why? A gamut of perplexing
emotions coursed through her. Joy, shock, anger, grief.
How could one be so giddily happy and so upset to see
someone at the same time?

How delighted her great-aunt was that Nat had
brought along his friend, and such a noble one at that. She
chattered the entire way to the mansion, interspersed by
Nat's anecdotes. Between the two of them chatting, there
was no need to talk at all.

Their carriage pulled up in front of a sweeping
mansion with Palladian pillars. Percy descended and held
out his hand to help her down the carriage steps. Frances
hesitated, but then snubbed his helping hand and
descended on her own, lifting her skirt in one hand and
holding the handle of the door in the other. She felt his
gaze between her shoulders when she turned her back
to him.

Dinner at the Westington Mansion wasn't any better.
She had no appetite at all and picked at the food on her
plate. Percy, being an earl, was seated far away from her,
next to the host. Yet she felt her gaze drifting to him
repeatedly. More than once, their eyes met, and a jolt shot
through her body every time. Her table partner attempted
to converse with her about politics, which normally interested her, but now her mind was too frazzled to focus.

After dinner, the gentlemen retreated, leaving the ladies to themselves.

"Do you wish to go home?" her great-aunt asked abruptly. "I couldn't help but notice that there seems to be something between you and Halsford. If you'd rather not be here, you need but say the word. Besides, our objective has been achieved. I have Lady Lieven's vouchers for Almack's." She smiled triumphantly.

Frances squeezed her hand gratefully. "I am afraid it will be impolite of us to remove ourselves so soon."

"Yes, there is some entertainment planned. Give it an hour. I wait for your sign."

She could have hugged her great-aunt on the spot.

After the gentlemen returned, there were to be performances. Frances ensconced herself in a chair in a corner, prepared to wait through the rest of the evening.

Then they set up the piano, and chairs around it, and Frances knew with a sense of dread what would come next.

"My daughter Elizabeth is a most excellent player. Let her talent entertain you," Lady Winterbottom's shrill voice rang out.

"As is Mary. She can play the clavichord like no other," piped up another woman's voice.

"Esther can play the harp. Do we have a harp?"

"How about a quartet with violins? Surely Emma isn't the only one who can play violin. It is a most superior instrument."

"I would like to hear Miss Littleworth sing." The calm, authoritative voice of the earl had the effect of immediately shutting down all other requests.

"Excellent notion." Polly nodded in approval.

"I daresay my sister can sing a pleasant tune," Nat contributed.

Frances glared at poor Nat, as if it were his fault she had to sing.

"What?" he mouthed at her, shrugging his shoulders.

All eyes were on her. Frances knew that resistance was futile. Like in a dream, she got up, walked over to the pianino, sat down, and placed her fingers on the ivory keys.

She did not need any music sheets. She closed her eyes, searched for the music, and sang.

Greensleeves.

The music transported her back to the seminary. To a long, cold winter's night. To a crackling fire in the fireplace, the smell of holly and mistletoe and mulled cider.

And the knowledge that her singing brought joy to someone she cared for deeply.

She sang only that one song. The applause was long and sincere, and she received many compliments on her way back to her seat. She smiled, nodded, smiled again. She avoided his eyes.

The room was too hot, the emotions too strong.

She needed to get away.

While Miss Winterbottom hammered on the piano, singing a ballad in a strained, shrill voice, Frances slipped out of the room.

The air on the balcony was fresh, and she was glad she'd brought her shawl. Several lamps were lit outside. Only a few moments, she told herself, then she'd return.

"I'm sorry," a familiar baritone voice said behind her.

She froze. Of course. He'd had to follow her.

"You are sorry again? What for? That you lied to me?

Or that you made me sing just now?" Her voice had a small hitch.

"Both." His voice was low. From the sound of it, he'd come closer. She could feel the heat of his body. She trembled, and it was not from the cold.

"Do you know that just the mere memory of your singing was what kept me sane all these months? What wouldn't I have given to hear your voice again."

She did not turn around but clasped her shawl about her throat with quivering fingers.

"Frances. Will you not talk to me?" His voice was pleading. "Will you not tell me how things are at the seminary?"

Frances finally turned. He stood slightly bent, his eyes boring into hers. "It is not an exaggeration to say that these few weeks at the seminary have been the happiest in my entire life. I have missed everything about it since I left."

Frances rubbed a finger along the marble pattern of the balustrade. "The students certainly have missed you. No one has been a better instructor of the fine arts. And Miss Hilversham still hasn't found a replacement."

"How is everyone there? How are the students?"

She told him briefly about the changes that had been implemented at the seminary, which students had left, which had come, and general news about the school.

A wistful look crossed his face. "Is the mural still there?"

"Of course it is. The girls have insisted on completing it. It looks quite the thing. Even Miss Hilversham approves." A small smile flitted over her face.

"I am glad." He looked up at the night sky, as if

studying the stars. "It is good to know I left a mark there, however small."

"You should continue painting and show your talent to the world," Frances said. "You ought to exhibit your work."

He leaned his elbows on the balcony and sighed. "How? Mr Tiverton can be an artist and a drawing master. In the eyes of society, that is acceptable. But an earl?"

Ah yes. He was a lord now. She kept forgetting.

"Why?" Her voice was a whisper. "Why didn't you just tell me?" Why hadn't he trusted her? The question had gnawed at her during sleepless nights.

"Why would it have mattered? Would you have hired a viscount and heir to an earldom as a drawing master? Would you have trusted him more than plain Mr Tiverton, amateur artist and teacher? I rather think you would've pushed me away either way."

Frances cringed. Was he right? She found no reply to that.

"I did not think that I was deceiving anyone maliciously, Frances. I am more Mr Tiverton than I am the earl." He spoke in a low voice. "The title, the inheritance, my role, an engagement. I thought I could go along with it if I only had my art. But my father, he forbade me to paint. I refused. We had a row." He flexed his hands. "He threatened to cut me off. I told him it didn't matter. I could survive on my own. I wanted, no, I needed to prove that I could fend for myself on my own. And I did."

"I read the obituary in the newspaper. He died of heart failure." Frances looked at him with sorrow.

"They say it was because of shock and grief. Because I left. It is like I killed him."

"Percy!" Frances's hand crawled to her throat. "That is not true. It wasn't your fault."

"Wasn't it?" His voice was laced with bitterness. "He may be still alive if I'd bowed to his strictures, taken on the seat in parliament and married Sophia. Will you believe me when I tell you I as good as forgot about our engagement when I was at the seminary? Probably not. It was never a love match." He swallowed, and his Adam's apple bobbed in his throat. "We are no longer engaged, by the way."

She did not know what to say. So, he was not to marry Sophia after all. She did not feel any relief or happiness, only confusion.

"Sophia ended the engagement when she realised I love someone else." He took a step forward.

Frances's eyes flew up to him.

"Someone without whom I can't seem to live." Percy took another step forward. "Or breathe."

He was awfully close.

She wanted to run. She wanted to stay. A hot ache grew in her throat. She tilted her face up.

He crushed her to him. This kiss wasn't gentle. It set the pit of her stomach to a wild swirl. For a long while, she ceased thinking.

"Frances, my love," he murmured against her lips. "Marry me."

Just say yes, her heart urged. Say yes and finally be at peace.

But her mind, that logical, reasonable organ, listed all the reasons why that was impossible. She was a schoolteacher. He was an earl. She was needed at the seminary. He was needed in this glittering society world that she had no part in. Earls did not marry schoolteachers. His world was not hers.

And yet. Did any of it really matter in the face of love?

Then a whisper rose from the depths of her being, that age-old whisper, familiar and malicious. *He's already betrayed you once.*

They always tell you they love you. Before they leave.

Like Father.

It stuck like a poisonous dart in the very depth of her soul.

She untangled herself from his arms. "Do not speak of love or marriage to me, my lord."

"Frances." His voice broke.

She turned her back to him and shook her head. She could not, would not see his face.

"I can't marry you. Ever. I'm sorry."

It took all her willpower to walk away from him.

CHAPTER 18

*F*rances was fine.

Really, she was.

She kept herself so busy that she had no time to think about anything at all. Least of all about him. There were so many things to see in London. The Tower and Vauxhall. The Egyptian Hall. Operas and plays in the evening, not to speak of all those balls and dinners. Her great-aunt had set up an exhausting schedule of entertainment. In between balls and routs, they took walks in the park with Prinny. The dog, not the Prince Regent.

She always braced herself prior to a social event, lest she meet him again. Yet since that fateful night, they had not crossed paths. She did not know whether to be relieved or disappointed.

"One wonders where Halsford has disappeared to once more," she heard a gentleman say at a dinner party. "He is neither at the clubs nor at any of the balls. I heard he tends to do that. Run away whenever he sees it fit. Disappear into thin air."

"Maybe he is travelling?" suggested Lady Millford, who was disappointed to have lost a possible suitor for her three daughters.

The gentleman who uttered those words took a pinch of snuff. "Who knows? They say he disappeared for months on end last winter. Not even the bow street runners could find him. Only to reappear out of nowhere to claim his inheritance when his father died."

Frances bit on her lips to refrain from a sharp retort. She was glad when her great-aunt suggested they leave. It had been a tiresome evening.

"As much as I loathe having to press you, and I'd rather you told me out of your own volition, I feel I need to probe what is the matter," her aunt said in the carriage on the way home. "Those rings around your eyes are not good. Neither is that sad countenance of yours. In short. What is the matter?"

"I received a proposal from Lord Halsford, and I declined. That's all."

"That's all?" Her great-aunt threw up her hands. "My dear, sweet child. Whatever on earth has induced you to turn down his proposal?"

"Common sense, Polly. He is an earl. I am a school-teacher. Earls and schoolteachers don't marry. End of story."

"Balderdash."

"Excuse me?"

"I said, balderdash. You may be a schoolteacher by profession, but you are every bit as worthy to be his bride as any other lady. You are of good stock. Never let it be said otherwise."

"Great-aunt Polly." Frances rubbed her eyes tiredly.

"Look at what happened to my parents. And there, the social gap wasn't nearly as great as it is with me and Halsford."

"What nonsense is this? And don't great-aunt Polly me. I won't have it. Listen to me. Whatever happened to your parents was their own responsibility. It has nothing to do with you. You come from a proud lineage of barons. Your grandfather was married to a duke's daughter. *Her* sister was the mistress of George II." She pulled herself up, proudly. "So you see, our family has a liaison with the Hanovers, which means we have a connection to the king himself."

"Aunt! I mean, Polly," Frances laughed. "I am not certain this is something to be proud of."

"Of course it is. Never let it be said that you are a mere schoolteacher, because it simply isn't true. You are worthy to marry an earl."

Frances sighed. "Be that as it may. I declined him and that's it."

"A great pity. He seemed to be greatly in love with you."

"Great-aunt!" Frances shot out of her seat.

"Sit down. You will never learn to call me Polly, will you?" She sighed. "Though come to think of it, maybe it is better you don't marry him after all."

This also nettled Frances. "And why this sudden change of mind?"

"He is giving up far too easily. So you gave him a basket. He backs down and licks his wounds. Pshaw. His affections can't be very deep after all. What a shame. Come, Prinny. We will go to the park and let her ponder on this."

. . .

IN THE END, IT WAS FRANCES WHO TOOK PRINNY TO THE
park, with her great-aunt's words rotating in her mind.
Truth was, she doubted everything. Especially her
emotions. She was simply not herself these days.

Neither was Prinny. He was uncommonly active,
pulling her across the meadow towards the yew bushes,
sniffing around as if it was the most exciting pastime ever.

"Why, Prinny, since when are you so athletic?" Frances
could barely keep up with him as he ran towards a poodle
who sat prettily next to a young lady who wore an
exquisite sky-blue walking dress with lace, ribbons and
flounces. She stared at Frances in such an outright way
that Frances wondered whether she had a smudge on her
cheek. She rubbed it with a gloved finger.

"Forgive me for apprehending you like this. You may
think my behaviour to be excessively bad mannered." The
young woman kept staring into her face.

Frances's eyes widened as she recognised her. She
clenched the reticule between her hands. "We have met
before. You are Miss Sophia Fielding."

"Yes. But I am sorry, I do not recall your name."

"Frances Littleworth."

"Frances Littleworth," the young woman echoed. "So
it is."

Both ladies curtsied to each other. Poodle and Prinny
sniffed at each other tentatively, then decided they were
in love.

"Would you mind very much if we walked together?"
Sophia threw a glance at her party. "I am certain the
others will wait for me."

"Very well." Prinny danced about Poodle, evidently delighted to spend more time with his newfound love.

"Shall we walk over to that bench under yonder trees?" Sophia suggested, pointing to a group of trees. "It is lovely that I can finally talk to you."

"Is it?"

"Why, yes. I have known Percy since we were children. Our fathers affianced us to each other without caring about the exact nature of our emotions. And who knows, maybe our marriage would have been a good one." She picked a daisy and stared at it. "Or not."

Frances listened silently, her mind a whirl of over-heated thoughts.

Sophia leaned forward. "I will tell you something. Percy doesn't know that I know this. Ever since he was little, there was nothing he wanted more than to be an artist. He'd dreamed of schools elsewhere, where they did not think art was useless. There was one in Paris, L'Ecole des Beaux Arts. There was one even closer, in London, even. The Royal Academy of Arts. They trained young artists and held annual exhibitions of their artwork. He talked of nothing else.

His father would have none of it. Drawing was one thing. But exhibiting in public? The son of an Earl? He was to go to Cambridge and study law. Like he himself did, like his grandfather had done. And like his own son would do one day, too. So, he collected all of Percy's drawings and burned them."

"No!" Frances gasped.

"That almost broke him. He went to Cambridge. He tried, he really did. Because he wanted to please his father, he gave in to his father's wishes and failed miserably. His tutors complained he was too dreamy and consistently skipped classes. Before they expelled him altogether, Percy had quit on his own."

"He is one of the kindest people I know," Sofia continued. "It is just that we don't love each other. We are fond of each other like brother and sister are. But we can't ever be in love."

"But he abandoned you," Frances stammered. "He ran away."

Her eyes widened when Sophia shrugged.

"I do not see it like that. I am glad he left. It was time he broke free from his father's strictures. He went to find himself, and he did exactly that. What's more, he met you."

Frances flushed. "I think you misunderstand the nature of our relationship. Ours is, or rather, was, a strictly professional relationship."

They sat down on the bench under the trees.

"He was rather distracted when he returned. Of course, that was also because his father just passed away so suddenly. But there was also another reason. It wasn't until recently that I noticed that Percy's affections were lying elsewhere. He is clearly in love with you."

Frances looked at her in anguish. "You must dislike me excessively."

"Nonsense. Why should I? I wish for Percy to be happy, as I am certain he wishes for me. It is good for Percy to be in love. But, you, see," a wistful look crossed Sophia's face, "I too deserve to be in love. I do not want to be tied to someone who doesn't love me, you see. For a while, I thought I could be satisfied with what we had. But," she shook her head. "I also realised I want more."

Frances stared at the daisy petals on the ground, which Sophia had plucked into pieces, not knowing what to say.

"So, it is for the best. We are still friends, Percy and I. That is a bond no one can take."

"I am glad to hear that," Frances whispered.

"Only one question remains." Sophia's gaze was solemn.

"Which one?"

"Do you love him?"

She felt Sophia's questioning eyes on her.

It was such a simple question. Yet Frances did not know how to answer.

Why was her heart hammering like it was about to jump out of her chest?

"Of course—not," she stammered.

Sophia looked at her sadly. "What a pity. Poor Percy deserves someone who loves him back. Maybe you will change your mind?"

Frances did not reply.

Sophia pulled herself up and looked back. "Well. I better return. They are waiting for me. Thank you for walking with me. It has been a pleasure meeting you, Miss Littleworth. Come, Serafina," she called the poodle.

Frances nodded woodenly and watched how Sophia walked back with her dog and rejoined her party.

"Come, Prinny, we will go back, too."

Do you love him?

The question echoed in her mind.

As she stood up and shook out her dress, she repressed the thought that she'd nearly, so very nearly, had replied with an affirmative.

CHAPTER 19

$\mathcal{F}$rances wanted to go home.

Home—that was the seminary in Bath. She wanted to return to her students, who missed her, and whom she missed as well. To Miss Hilversham, who held a strict rein over the school. Life there was predictable and safe. Her days were busily scheduled from dawn to dusk, and there was no room for thinking about certain tall men with kind twinkles in their eyes.

Polly hadn't wanted to let her go. Neither had Nat. Both had talked, wheedled, cajoled her into staying in London.

"There are still so many balls to attend! And a ridotto at Vauxhall!"

Frances insisted. In the end, Polly had relented. "I am the last one to force you to stay, child. I wish you would change your mind."

"It is for the best. I would love to return next summer, maybe."

"Nat, of course, will have to return to Cambridge. I will keep a strict eye on him, never fear."

Nat's behaviour had much improved, and he seemed to have found his way back to his books again.

"You worked miracles with this boy. What did you tell him to bring about this change?" Frances asked.

Polly smiled. "It is easy. I told him he would be my heir."

Frances gasped. "But, Polly. Are you certain?"

"Provided he finishes his studies within this year." She tapped her little silver snuffbox and took a pinch. "I will also cover all his expenses. On the condition he excels in his exams. Then, he has a profession at this law firm waiting for him. You will stop paying for the boy and refuse him when he comes asking for money."

"Polly. You are more than generous. You are an angel."

"Nonsense. It is the least thing I can do for Charity's children. After all this time we wasted apart."

Frances slung her arms around her and hugged her tightly.

Polly gave her a quick squeeze, then untangled herself with a sniff.

Thus, Frances returned to Bath, relieved that her brother was taken care of, and she no longer needed to feel any pressure to maintain his lifestyle.

Maybe she'd imagined it, but had Miss Hilversham looked disappointed when she returned? She'd looked at Frances with a long, scrutinising look.

"I did not expect you back so soon," she'd said. It had sounded like she'd said, "I did not expect you to return at all."

But return she did.

She threw herself into a frenzy of activity that kept her so busy, she did not have time to think at all.

One day, she received a delivery from London. It was a packet from Polly.

I forgot to give you this box. It was your mother's, Polly wrote. *Since she is no more, this belongs to you. She visited me shortly before she passed, asking me to safe keep it for you.*

Frances inspected the box. It was pretty, inlaid with mother-of-pearl, and smelled of sandalwood. She laid the box on her bed and opened it.

It was full of letters.

Frances gasped when she recognised the handwriting.

They were from her father.

She rifled through them. There were many, easily hundreds of them. Starting from their courtship to the time when she was a little girl.

She read them breathlessly.

My love, how I wish you would join me here. Life is strenuous here in the colonies; yes, it is rough, but it is also more grounded. I have never been so close to nature as here. I have found a house, and I dream of you and the children. When will you finally join me? Write soon. I will never stop loving you and little Frances and little Nat...

Virginia 1797

Virginia? Frances could barely believe her eyes. What did this mean? Her father—had been in the colonies? She calculated. The date of the letter was long after that fateful Christmas when he left them.

Three years. She flipped through the letters. There were three years' worth of letters, each describing in great detail how he painstakingly attempted to build up a new life in the New World.

"I don't understand," Frances muttered. She rubbed her eyes.

He'd left for the colonies?

But why had her mother never told her this?

Why had her mother let them believe he abandoned her?

Frances clearly remembered that day when she asked her mother where her father was. Her mother was sitting in front of the window, staring outside with empty eyes. "He's left us." That was all she said. She never talked about her father again.

With a shaking hand, she pulled out one letter that was written in a different handwriting.

We regret to inform you that your husband, Edward Little-worth, has died in an accident last Friday, April 27, 1800...

Frances stared blindly at the letter.

She picked up the letters again and perused them for the third time. He always asked about the children. Full of yearning. Full of love.

She'd been so little. Could it be... that she simply hadn't registered the bag he may have had slung over his shoulder before he left? Could it be that she simply hadn't understood when they'd talked about him leaving? She remembered them arguing. She remembered her mother weeping.

Frances put her hand on her forehead.

"Oh, mother," she whispered, "If only you'd talked more to me about father."

For her mother had never mentioned him again. She had not wanted to join him. To her, he'd abandoned them.

She'd been wrong, so very wrong.

Her father had never abandoned them.

He never stopped loving her.

Tears flowed.

Tears of regret. Of terrible sadness.

Of healing.

CHAPTER 20

ime passed so quickly when one was busy. Before Frances knew, Christmas was approaching. The fragrant smell of cinnamon, orange peel and almonds that infused the entire house indicated that Mrs Beedle was busily preparing plum pudding. It became a great sport amongst the students to steal into the pantry and snatch away pieces of the pudding when she wasn't looking.

"The next person I catch will receive a raw onion in her mince pie," Mrs Beedle threatened, to the delight of the children.

Frances was getting a tad bit dreamy and nostalgic. On St Thomas day, exactly a year ago, he'd arrived. How long ago that had been. She remembered how it had snowed that day. This year, however, there was no sign of snow. That was only for the best, Frances told herself. The faster she could forget, the better. Except try as she might, her heart refused to forget.

On Christmas eve, they hung out the greenery, the

mistletoe and holly. This year, there were three students staying at the seminary over Christmas, as well as most of the staff. Everyone was thankfully healthy, and Mrs Beedle had sworn to make up for last year's Christmas, so she cooked, grilled, pickled, baked and stewed as if for an army.

Miss Hilversham and the other teachers were invited to Mrs Benningfield's Christmas dinner at the Grand Manor. The invitation had been extended to her as well, but Frances decided to remain behind and finish her work.

"You intend to work on Christmas eve?" Miss Hilversham lifted a finely plucked eyebrow.

"If I finish it all now, I will enjoy the holidays even more afterwards, with only relaxation to look forward to." This is what she'd told them. The reality was that she did not want to ruin the memory of magic she had of the place, of a time she was truly happy. She did not want to see the kissing bough hanging in the door of the ballroom, which reminded her of a promise that was never kept.

Frances hung up the last holly wreath on the wall above the fireplace and stared down at the last mistletoe bough, wishing she were less melancholic, when someone rapped on the door.

It must be another mumper, Frances thought. "Never mind, Martha, I will get the door." She took off her apron and opened the door.

"The thing is this," he said as he turned. His greatcoat fluttered in the wind, and his eyes sparkled with emotion. "The thing is that I've thought quite a bit in the meantime."

Frances leaned against the doorframe in a rush of giddiness. He'd come. Heavens! He'd come.

"Oh, did you," she choked.

"Yes." His eyes devoured her.

"And you had to come here all the way from London to tell me you've had time to think?" She gripped the door between her hands, afraid it was all a dream. "After five months?"

"One-hundred-and-fifty-two days, to be exact. You see, I counted every day, every minute apart."

"You could've written a letter?" she whispered.

"I did not think a letter would do it justice. Sometimes you just have to say things in person." They stood, staring at each other, while the wind blew into the house.

"What is it you wanted to say?"

The wind tousled his hair and brought colour to his cheeks. "That I've taken time to heal. To think. To get my life in order. I came to some conclusions, Frances. And I had to share them with you."

Frances opened the door. "Come in then. It is getting rather cold standing here."

He followed her inside. He stopped in front of the mural, which the students had completed, and studied it in silence.

"What do you think?" Frances could not tear her gaze away from him. The Gods of Olympus were complete, as were the heroes of mythology.

"This is exceptionally good." He beamed at her. "Don't you think? How well they completed the task."

"You can be proud," Frances said softly. "Both in what you accomplished with the students, and what you created yourself."

Frances poured tea in the drawing room, and it was as though he'd never been away, with the familiar sight of him lounging in the armchair by the fireplace. He looked around, clearly pleased to be back. "How I have missed this place. Tell me what you have been doing in the meantime, Frances Littleworth."

"I, too, have thought quite a bit," Frances told him. "Mainly about my childhood." She found herself telling him about her father. She hadn't told anyone, so it was a relief to share this with someone.

He listened gravely. "It appears your mother was so caught up in her own world of pain that she never noticed what you went through. You took on her feelings and beliefs about your father. And you did not understand what was really happening."

"How could I? I was but a child. Sometimes I wonder if I would have made different decisions in my life, had I known that my father never really abandoned us."

Percy brightened at those words. "That is heartening to hear. Very heartening indeed." He jumped up and rubbed his hands. "Miss Littleworth."

"Mr Tiverton?"

"You're not, by any chance, in need of a drawing master?"

Frances shook her head regretfully. "That position is already filled, I'm afraid."

"Ah. That is a shame. What about a history teacher? Surely, you must need a history teacher. One who knows for a fact that William the Conqueror landed in England in ten-sixty-six."

Frances choked back a laugh and shook her head.

"Latin? No?" He ruffled his hair in mock despair. "I

shall be a patron, then. I will be the most generous patron the school has ever had. I will rent the house next door with the wishing well. And I will come and inspect the school on a weekly, no, daily basis to check whether the current drawing master is doing his job properly. And, of course, to see one teacher in particular…"

Her hand crawled to her throat. "As far as I know, Miss Hilversham never declines a sponsor."

"Ah, it is not for Miss Hilversham I would do this. But to prove I am a particularly generous sponsor, once in a while I might invite the entire school to come visit the Royal Academy of Arts exhibition in London. Particularly this coming spring."

"Percy!" Frances gasped. "You are exhibiting there?"

He grinned. "I am studying there. Someone told me I ought to exhibit my work more, you see. And I have decided it does not matter what they say. Whether it is appropriate or not. One day, I have vowed, I will teach there. I have worked furiously. Five of my paintings are to be on display. Under the name P.B. Tiverton."

"Oh Percy, this is wonderful. I am very happy for you."

"Yes. And do you know what my masterpiece is?" He stepped towards her.

Frances rose.

"It is a painting called 'The Muse'." He gently lifted her chin with his finger and studied her face with curious intensity.

"The Muse," she repeated breathlessly.

"Yes."

She could not tear her gaze away from his face.

"You see, I realise I have been a bit of a fool," he said huskily. "When I proposed to you that night, and you said you couldn't marry me. It never occurred to me to ask why not. I am such an idiot. I thought it was because you didn't return my feelings, but I think—I think—I may have been mistaken. An encounter with your great-aunt convinced me I must be the biggest buffoon in the universe."

"Polly?" She looked up, surprised.

"She is a force of nature, your great-aunt. She berated me heavily for giving up so easily. I decided she was right."

Frances closed her eyes and swayed.

"Mr Tiverton," she whispered.

"Miss Littleworth." Her heart turned over at the longing in his eyes. "Was I mistaken about your feelings? Tell me. I must know."

"Yes, you were mistaken," Frances whispered. Then she pulled herself up. "The truth is… the truth is that I've loved you… since you stood in your shirt and stockinged feet in front of me, half-ill, demanding an interview." Frances chuckled at the memory. "I just didn't know my heart."

Percy's face broke out into a smile that brought tears of happiness into her eyes. He looked up, searching the empty door frame above. "Where the deuce is the mistletoe when one needs it? Never mind. Because I am about to repeat that mistletoe promise, regardless. Listen closely, Frances Littleworth."

She placed a finger against his lips. "Hush. Now it is my turn to say it, Percy Tiverton." She held his face between her hands as she repeated the words he'd told her that night. "*I will love you till the end of time.*"

Percy lifted her up, whirled her around, and kissed her.

Outside the window, first one, then two sluggish snowflakes floated down, followed by several more, until suddenly an entire host whirled about, culminating in a wild, happy dance.

Christmas has come.

~

ABOUT THE AUTHOR

Sofi was born in Vienna, grew up in Seoul, studied Comparative Literature in Maryland, U.S.A., and lived in Quito with her Ecuadorian husband. When not writing, she likes to scramble about the countryside exploring medieval castle ruins, which she blogs about here. She currently lives with her husband, 3 trilingual children, a sassy cat and a cheeky dog in Europe.

Get in touch and visit Sofi at her Website, on Facebook or Instagram!

- a amazon.com/Sofi-Laporte/e/B07N1K8H6C
- f facebook.com/sofilaporteauthor
- twitter.com/Sofi_Laporte
- instagram.com/sofilaporteauthor
- BB bookbub.com/profile/sofi-laporte

ALSO BY SOFI LAPORTE

The Wishing Well Series
Lucy and the Duke of Secrets
Arabella and the Reluctant Duke
Birdie and the Beastly Duke
Penelope and the Wicked Duke

Wishing Well Seminary Series
Miss Hilversham and the Pesky Duke

A Regency Christmas
A Mistletoe Promise

Merry Spinsters, Charming Rogues Series
Lady Ludmilla's Accidental Letter

Made in the USA
Coppell, TX
29 June 2024

34079327R00104